Where polarities integrate and forgiveness facilitates oneness

The intertwined evolutionary romantic journey of two strangers

AATMN PARMAR

INDIA • SINGAPORE • MALAYSIA

ISBN 979-8-88869-962-1

Phone No.: +919833402657
Website: www.aatmn.com
https://www.facebook.com/ParmarAatmn
https://twitter.com/aatmnparmar
https://www.instagram.com/aatmn/
https://www.linkedin.com/in/aatmn/

Dedicated to my Mother and Father
Mrs. Sudha Ramesh Parmar
Mr. Ramesh Devchand Parmar

Disclaimer

This is a work of fiction. Names, characters, business, events and incidents are the products of the Author's imagination. Any resemblance to actual persons (living or dead), or actual events is purely coincidental. This book is written with the desire to create awareness of integration of spirituality with human aspirations.

Gratitude

One fine day, sitting in a hotel lobby in Singapore, I started writing with my eyes closed and fingers tapping on the keyboard, not knowing what I was writing.

In a matter of half an hour, I had typed the first chapter. In the next 7 days, almost all my scheduled appointments uncannily got canceled and my first book was born.

When I re-read the book, I realized that unknowingly I had written about the Chakra Evolution, without making it obvious. Learning can be with ease, grace, and fun. A deep Chakra Philosophy was gifted to us by channeled writing in an interesting story form.

My second book, Redikall Crystalline Mind, would explain how channeled writing works.

Chakras are powerful energy centers. Apart from 250+ known minor chakras as described in the Redikall Curriculum, we have the well-known, 7 Major Chakras. They are the First Chakra or the Root Chakra, which inspires us to survive and thrive; the Second Chakra is the Sacral Chakra, which inspires us to enjoy life; the Third Chakra, Solar Plexus Chakra, inspires us to rise beyond power games and need for control; the Heart Chakra inspires us to forgive and flow and be a channel of love; the Fifth Chakra, Throat Chakra inspires us to believe in ourselves and recognise who we are; The Third Eye Chakra inspires us to implement all our dreams, ideas and visions; and the Crown Chakra which inspires us to seek oneness and experience the divinity in all that is.

Spiritual growth takes you through these phases of life and when that happens the experience of bliss is inevitable.

I urge you to read this book at least twice. Once like a storybook and later to grasp the deeper philosophy embedded in the text and quotes.

Later, as and when you are in need of some guidance, you can simply open the book and your eyes will go to the message precisely meant for you in that moment.

It is channeled writing. The characters are fictitious. Any resemblance is purely co- incidental. I do not claim the thoughts and quotes to be mine. They are relevant to the chapter and they have been written in a channeled space. Some of them may resemble pre-existing quotes. However, there is no deliberate attempt to copy anyone's work through this book.

This book was written way back in 2010 and published under a different name and title. On popular demand, I am reprinting the same work with minor changes in some of the pages.

A deep gratitude to all my team members who have given me unconditional support and love.

And of course, deep reverence to the unseen frequencies, who wrote this book through me. May this book make you experience the bliss of Eternal Enlightenment.

Happy Reading!
Aatmn Parmar

About the Author

Aatmn Parmar is the Founder of Redikall - a revolutionary method of easing life through consciousness expansion. This amazing collection of principles and copyrighted techniques is a gift to humanity with the precious channeled knowledge of 250+ minor chakras. Redikall has transformed many lives and has brought about a positive lifestyle shift.

Aatmn is the author of many books; the most popular ones are Redikall Crystalline Mind and Hello! This Is Money Speaking. She conducts training programs and workshops in several countries and influences people across the globe with her online courses.

The Beginning of the End

"On behalf of Captain Sodhi and the crew members, we welcome you aboard the Indian Airlines flight IA 107 from Delhi to Mumbai. Kindly adjust your seats to an upright position and fasten your seat belts as we prepare for take-off."

The announcement broke Sarah, out of her reverie. She was looking visibly upset and depressed.

Hopefully, this flight represents a new take-off in my life, she thought, sighing with relief, as she fastened her seat belt.

Hope is like a mirage enticing you to continue moving forward in times of utter despair.

Many people succumb to the sorrows of life out of hopelessness. She tried gifting herself some hope, but the state of despair continued to grip her emotions and the battle inside her mind became more fierce with every passing moment.

Every new moment in our lives gifts us a fresh opportunity to be different. The question is: Do we really want to change?

Just three hours ago, on the way to the airport, she had been robbed of all the money she had been carrying from the U.S. She wanted to trust the world, but she did not know whom to trust. Her jolted faith made her look at everyone around, including the cabin crew, with suspicion. A part of her wanted to go back home to the USA, the country where she was born and had grown up.

Yet, another part of her did not know what she would do if she went back there. Her mind drifted back to that fateful day when she had declared to her father her intention to go to India.

"What nonsense!" her father had blasted. "India is a country full of snake charmers, thieves, rogues and terrorists. That's where you wanna go?" He had protested in outrage. When she reiterated her resolve to go there, her father had practically disowned her.

"You will come back heart-broken," were the last words of her father, as she finally hugged him at the airport.

I won't prove him right. I won't go back like this. "No, No, No..." the last few words inadvertently slipped out of her mouth, drawing the attention of her co-passenger.

He asked, "Sorry, did you say something to me?"

Instantly, Sarah came back to her current reality and turned cautiously to face a pair of large dark eyes staring at her. "Hi, I am Arun, Arun Deshmukh from Bombay.... Sorry Mumbai."

He looked at her deep-sea green eyes. She seemed lost. Is she here or somewhere else? He wondered, watching her stare back at him.

At times, the most deafening experience is not the noise, but the silence.

Arun waited patiently. He knew that Sarah was struggling to get back to the present. Arun chose to stare at her intensely, making the silence terribly awkward for Sarah. Finally, she opened her mouth with great difficulty. "I'm Sarah."

Arun realized that she was too preoccupied to talk, so he did not push the onversation forward. He quietly returned to the in-flight magazine and started flipping through its pages, pretending to be interested in its mediocre masala.

Thank God! She was relieved that her co-passenger was sensitive enough to understand her need for privacy. She needed that time to be by herself.

Digesting unpleasant experiences of life is a great challenge because our mind has no specific excretory system devised to discard the unwanted.

Her mind had taken a good amount of time to process what had happened when she was on her way to the airport. She found herself slipping back in time to that fateful taxi drive.

"Madam are you holding a valid license for the revolver that you have in your purse?" demanded the taxi driver in his typical North Indian accent.

"What? Nonsense! A revolver? In my purse? R r r r r..uuuubbish!" She exclaimed in disbelief and agitation.

"Check your purse madam, it is very much there." He smirked. She hesitatingly opened up the purse and was aghast to find the revolver. All of a sudden, the taxi stopped right outside a police station.

Sarah had had her fair share of unpleasant experiences in the past few months as she had traveled extensively in India. But to be branded as a criminal was simply unthinkable!

"Oh no! I can't believe this. Can you help me? I'm innocent, it isn't mine." She tried to throw the revolver.

The taxi driver smiled at her and said, "Madam, don't do that. The revolver now has your fingerprints on it. And that is enough to get you arrested."

"Wh...wh...what should I do now?" stammered a completely shocked and confused Sarah.

"I could save you Madam, but it is a big risk, you know! And what will I get out of it?"

"What do you want?"

"Give me all your money," said the taxi driver with a straight and serious face.

"Ohh!" Slowly reality dawned on her and she asked him helplessly, "So you did this for money?"

"Maybe, but how will you prove it? This is my country, and all these policemen are my friends. If you want, you could stay in jail with all your money. The choice is yours," he challenged.

She stared at him dumbfounded. There was very little time left. She would miss her flight if she got delayed any longer and with that would evaporate the precious opportunity to meet Guru Atmanandji, that charismatic personality, whom she considered to be the lighthouse, illuminating her spiritual path.

The money isn't so important anyway. What was important, however, was her mission to find her guru in India.

Poor dad, he has been picking up all the credit card bills so far. I guess he will have to put up with some more.

She took out the bundle of notes from her purse and handed it over to him reluctantly.

He said, "Give me your video camera and the watch." She was desperate to get out of the taxi by now.

Immediately, she handed over whatever he had asked for and got out of the taxi with her backpack and purse. Luckily for her, she realized that the revolver was still in her purse. She hastily removed it and clumsily cleaned it with a tissue hoping that her fingerprints would be erased. Disgusted, she threw the revolver back through the open window of the taxi.

"Bloody bastard!" She fumed as the taxi sped away in front of her eyes.

Fortunately, she still had her phone, which he either did not notice or was not interested in.

Her hand went to her pocket to check for any remnant Indian currency, and while counting the coins and notes she flagged down another cab to go to the airport.

There is always a way out, no matter where you are stuck. If you do not find the solution or a direction, inspect your need or desire to move on in your life.

She managed to reach the airport safely. As she cleared the taxi bill with the change in her pocket, she sighed with relief at having escaped the experience of an Indian prison and the police. Although all this had happened a while ago, the effect of the incident and its repercussions were still very fresh in her mind. As she took another deep sigh, tears started rolling down her face.

She remembered her father's face and felt guilty for wasting his money in such a manner. Although Dad did not mind her spending money on discos, bars, parties and clothes, he did not favor this bizarre pursuit of 'spirituality'.

"Excuse me, Ma'am," the air hostess offered her a wet cotton towel to freshen up.

For Sarah, the cool feel of the wet towel on her face seemed like a loving and reassuring pat from God.

In retrospect, you always realize the appropriateness of various events of the past.

She remembered Swami Sanmukhanandji mentioning this, in one of his discourses that she had listened to. If that was the case, was losing money in such a manner also the right thing at the right time? She questioned herself.

After listening to so many gurus during her stint of the last eight months with them, her confusion about spirituality was at its peak. She had amassed far too many intellectual concepts and was now beginning to wonder whether she had truly understood and imbibed anything at all from them. Had any of these concepts really elevated her life in any manner whatsoever? Everyone seemed to be contradicting each other to a certain extent. Every guru had left her with more questions. She had become a spiritual addict.

The sense of incompletion is directly proportional to the inflow of information, because the soul chooses to have the experience and not information.

Eight long months ago, she had started her journey with only one question: "Who is my Guru?" After all this while, in what now seemed like an eternity, she realized that she still had too many questions and, of course, her very first query remained unanswered.

We remain under an illusion of movement in life until the time life takes a full circle and brings us back to the point from where we started our journey, only to begin yet another compelling round of peregrination.

By now, she was feeling completely devastated and confused. She had never felt like this ever before.

Some more tears.... and some more sobs....

Suddenly, she became aware of her co-passenger's presence. Arun was observing her with a questioning look in his eyes. There were deep furrows between his eyebrows.

She quickly took out tissues from her purse and wiped her tears. "Sorry," she murmured.

"Sorry for what?" She kept quiet.

"You tend to use this word 'sorry' very often, isn't it?" he gently chided her.

She looked at him in astonishment with eyes wide open and almost involuntarily nodded her head in agreement.

"Looks like you are feeling sorry for yourself right now," he said.

He had managed to hit the nail on the most tender spot. Yes, that was exactly how it was. Lately, she had been feeling extremely sorry for herself. *How does he know?* she thought.

She had read that others know you much better in a moment, than you would know yourself in your lifetime. *How true!* she reflected. *Probably, all that I have done is feel sorry for myself and make my loved ones feel sorry for themselves and for me too. This has probably become my comfort zone...*

"Oh, how do you know that?" Her big eyes were looking at him for an answer now.

"Let me ask you the other way round. Have you observed anything about me so far?"

"Oh! Good question. Actually nothing. I was too busy with my own thoughts," said Sarah feeling sheepish.

"Shall I presume then that I am inconspicuous?" asked Arun.

She looked at him and blushed. "No, I am sorry, I did not mean that.... I mean..... I was too busy with myself to observe anyone around me."

"Did you notice the air hostess who gave you the wet towel and sweets?" asked Arun.

"Yes, she had a nice smile and lovely mahogany brown hair. Why are you asking me this?"

"She appeared in your life only for a few seconds and you noticed her. And here I am traveling with you, I probably have already spent a good thirty minutes in the seat next to you and you say you haven't noticed anything about me?" Arun continued emphatically. "This tells me your mind perceives me as inconspicuous."

This was very embarrassing for her. Here was a well-mannered, well dressed and good looking gentleman; next to whom she had spent the last half an hour or so, but yet had not observed anything about him.

"You are good looking, well dressed, your language is impeccable, and you appear to be kind. Besides, you read my mind very well." Sarah almost whispered the last few words, as if she were telling those to herself.

"Ah, that is your conscious mind analysis; your subconscious mind passed me off as someone who is inconspicuous." He smiled. She thought she had hurt him by her behavior. But no, looking at him, that did not appear to be the case. He appeared to be very calm about being unnoticed.

"Did you feel offended by my behavior? I am so sorry."

"Sorry again?" Both of them laughed. "Do you think you have taken up the challenge of keeping the entire world happy?"

"Not exactly." She felt embarrassed. "But yes, it is true that I am extremely sensitive to others' feelings. I try not to hurt them, but invariably end up doing just that."

The irony of life is that the experiences from which you try to escape, are the same experiences you invariably embrace.

Sarah felt quite vulnerable with this stranger, who seemed to be reading her through and through. She had been materially cheated in the morning, now she did not want to go through a similar experience at an emotional level with this mystical character.

As the air hostess started serving food, she sighed with relief. She felt as if the air hostess knew exactly how to reach out to her when she needed her the most. She was already experiencing butterflies in her stomach and felt the need to calm herself with food. In spite of understanding that the hunger might be false, all she wanted to do was to eat and gratify herself instantaneously.

She decided that she would not talk to this guy and would try her best to keep him off.

But would that kind of behavior hurt him? This is again a repetition of my pattern. I believe that I need to please and make everyone around me happy and knowingly or unknowingly I end up hurting, or at least making them unhappy. That's what I have done to my father. That's what I have done to my mother. In fact, I have done this at some time to everyone who has touched my life.

Sarah was busy introspecting.

Why do I keep behaving like that with everyone around me?

"You have a question in your mind that you are scared of asking, isn't it?" he intervened, breaking her chain of thought.

"Are you a mind reader?"

"Not at all. Look at your body language, the position of your fingers on your cheek, and the way you have your hand across your heart."

"Looks like you are afraid of being hurt again. Have you been hurt very badly in the past?" Arun wanted to know more about it.

There it goes...another bull's eye! How does he manage to keep hitting the nail on the right spot? I can't handle this anymore!

She decided to ignore him, so that she could follow the flow of her thoughts.

I wish I could hide all my feelings from this stranger. But I can't seem to. He is reading my thoughts by the minute. The last thing that I want to tell a stranger is the incident of being looted by a cab driver. Gosh! these tears in my eyes won't let me hide it anymore. I can't believe I am so transparent.

All these thoughts crossed her mind in a jiffy. The next few minutes could have put any soap opera to shame, as an excellent drama unfolded between the two of them. She described the horrifying experience she had gone through and how the incident had left her devastated.

As she started recovering from her deep sobs, she asked, "Tell me why did this happen to me? Why me?"

Our upbringing has taught us that only those who commit sins suffer in life. But when one suffers in spite of being ethical, the inward journey begins.

The first step in the evolution of a seeker's life is often marked by the question "Why me?"

"Because you invited it." Arun quickly replied, knowing fully well that it would be difficult for her to take it.

"Why would I invite this loot, this pennilessness? Why would I invite this shattering experience?"

"Ask yourself... ***There is always a payoff in every situation.***" Sarah was completely bewildered.

"But first things first, let me tell you, my observations. I see that you are finding it difficult to be in the present. If you were completely present and aware of yourself, you would have noticed the driver slipping the revolver into your purse."

She continued looking at him with her zapped expression. She had come across so many gurus in India, but nobody seemed to have pointed out this aspect. How true! That was the story of her life. In reaching out for higher aspirations, she had lost touch with her ground reality. Most of the people that she had met in various ashrams seemed to be suffering from the same problem. They could yap about Sanskrit Shlokas, concepts from the Gita, and all sorts of breath techniques to evolve the soul, but little did they know what was happening in the world around them. They were 'blissfully unaware'.

To rise higher in life, you need to reach deeper within.

"But I thought this is how one grows spiritually. Aren't we supposed to be detached from the worldly material things to attain 'Moksha'?"

"Detached? Yes. But ***there is a huge difference between being detached and being indifferent.***"

This one was still harder to take. "I beg your pardon? Do you see me as indifferent?"

"No, I perceive you as indifferent. ***The truth and its perception are not necessarily the same.***"

"What's the difference between being detached and being indifferent?" Sarah was now getting a little impatient with him.

"Indifference is an escape mechanism. It comes out of the perception of pain or simple disinterest in the world around. This could be a defense mechanism to protect one's own psyche, one's own emotions."

"Sorry, can you say that again? I still feel they are both similar, if not the same."

"Suppose you have a simple rash on your palm. If you are detached, you will be able to observe it neutrally, like a physician observing his patient's palm and doing the needful in a rational, logical and appropriate manner. But if you are operating out of a state of indifference, you will not bother about what is happening to your palm and why you attracted the rash on your palm. You will not even bother to take the appropriate steps to prevent further deterioration of the condition."

Arun continued. ***"Many spiritual seekers operate out of indifference rather than true detachment. When you are detached, there is no tendency to run away or give up or escape from anything in life. The neutrality that sets in because of the detachment, polishes you to attain the ultimate non-adhesiveness."***

"Do you own any property in India?" Sarah suddenly interrupted. "Yes."

"Explain to me with the example of your attitude towards your property.

How can you say whether you are attached, detached or indifferent to it?"

"Well, one of the properties that I own in India is an ancestral river-side farmhouse. If I am attached to it, I would be concerned about it all the time.

If I am indifferent to it, it would not matter to me whether it is well attended to and taken care of, or not. But when I look at the property in a detached manner, I become its custodian. I take great care of it until the time it is in my custody. ***With detachment it is easy to get the feeling of being a custodian of the belongings in one's life.***"

This started making more sense to Sarah than all the discourses she had heard so far.

"You're right. I tried running away from the pain, by searching for the 'truth'. That is what brought me to India. You mean to say I tried escaping the pain there, but life here will be equally painful?"

"Tell me Sarah, is it painful or is it full of suffering?"

" Well, I never thought about it. Let me think. It is mixed. Some parts of it are painful. Like today's incident has given me a lot of pain. The suffering might begin now, if the money is not arranged for by my father immediately. I have sent him a message on his cell phone. However, I will have to wait until he responds. Normally he is very generous about money matters, at least with me." Sarah was trying to reassure herself. Sarah appeared like a little baby who was trying to behave like a grown-up and mature adult.

"So, you do understand the difference between pain and suffering." the caring adult in Arun complimented her.

"Yes, to a certain extent. But tell me, can one avoid pain? Buddha said that pain is the truth of life."

"Well, ***even though pain is inflicted, suffering can be eliminated if consciousness is elevated.*** According to me all sufferings are the results of the feelings of guilt that we have."

"What? I don't have any guilt." "Sure?" asked Arun.

"Of course," replied Sarah emphatically.

"No guilt feelings, huh?" Arun questioned.

"I have committed no crime. I have murdered no one. I haven't robbed anyone. Why should I ever feel guilty?" She appeared very strong in her arguments.

You require courage to acknowledge the genuine feeling within.

"Do you think that one has to commit a legally impermissible act to feel guilty? With this logic all criminals would feel very guilty, but that's not the case." ***Criminals may not feel guilty after a majorly offensive act but conscientious ones feel terribly guilty over a trivial mistake.***

"Hmm, food for thought. I never thought of it that way."

"In fact, the most notorious criminals and terrorists have very justifiable reasons for their actions."

Then, when does one feel guilty?

"The guilt feeling could be out of the perception that you are not meeting your self-expectations."

"So, do you think I am feeling guilty because I haven't yet found a guru in India yet?"

"Not finding a guru in India could very well be your way of punishing yourself, for some other guilt feeling."

There he goes again. He can't be doing this to me. He is shooting bullets every minute with his pointed remarks. It is hitting me hard, and yet I am readily opening myself to him! Sarah wanted to keep quiet. She had taken more than she could handle from him.

"Ma'am, would you like to have some tea or a coffee?" Sarah gratefully shook her head, relieved as the air hostess once again interrupted an uncomfortable conversation at a very crucial point.

May God bless her for her excellent sense of timing! Is she a psychic? Or is someone up there taking care of me? I can now have some breathing time to think about what this stranger has told me. But wait a minute, is he a stranger? I can't handle this anymore. Too many assumptions. Too many questions. I was already confused, to begin with. He has confused me even more. Oh! I can't handle this splitting headache.

"Do you have a headache?"

She looked at him straight. But refrained from asking why he asked this question.

I am massaging my head, so obviously, he would presume that. "I am not asking because you have your fingers on your temples." "Then how do you know?"

"Too much confusion creates congestion at the temples. You see, when you feel guilty or not okay about yourself, the energy tends to get blocked at the throat level, creating further congestion in the body parts above the throat, and this perpetuates or aggravates the headache sooner or later." Now it was Sarah's turn to be amused as she watched him speak.

Wow, what compassionate grandfatherly wisdom, least expected from this young guy!

"You seem to have a logical answer to everything, all the time."

He chuckled, choosing to let the comment pass. *Am I trying to impress this babe by any chance? Although, I cannot deny that there is something about her that compels me to interact with her. She has not asked for help; she is not asking for sympathy and after all, I am not one of those 'gurus' that she is seeking out. What is it that is making me spend time on her? I am often proud of being a reserved person and now here I am busy for an hour, conversing with this girl, whom I don't know from anywhere! Interesting! Sounds like the beginning of a romantic story.*

Hey, this could be a good storyline. For such a long time, I have been looking out for some interesting subject to write about. Let's see what comes out of it. Probably this is the last time I am meeting her or probably not! What? Why am I even thinking on these lines? What happened to my habit of being in the 'now'? It's not like me to perch in the future like this.

"Well, now you seem to have gotten lost somewhere; I think you need to get more grounded. It is me who is in the present at this moment," she said with all her feminine charm.

This is uncanny. She is now picking up my thoughts. I can't believe this! I thought I was well shielded, and no one could decipher me. In fact, the fun of my life is to keep making everyone feel disillusioned about me, knowingly and deliberately. Anyway, I hope it is just a loose remark or one of those 'coincidences'. But there is nothing like a coincidence and I believe it firmly. Then in that case, why have I attracted her in my life?

"Wake up, Varun. It is time to get off."

"It is A-run," corrected Arun. *She is right. It is time for her to get off my mind,* he wound up his thoughts.

"I am so sorry, I will try and remember it," apologized Sarah for not addressing him correctly.

"What are you sorry for?"

Both of them had a hearty laugh. For a while, her headache seemed to have reduced a bit.

Sarah had very mixed feelings in her heart. Something within her had been stirred and shaken at all levels. She did not know how to react to this. One thing was definite - his style of questioning and commenting had helped her in getting more clarity.

Optimism and Pessimism are two sides of the same coin. A lot depends upon your perception based on your position.

There was a sense of optimism and at the same time a bit of desperation.

She knew she had much more to learn from him. But how would she find him? She didn't even know where he lived. Which town had he talked about?

He handed his business card to her as he ascended the steps on the airway bus.

This is amazing, I knew that thoughts manifest, but I did not know they would manifest so fast.

She thanked him and as the bus began to move, Sarah looked around for a vacant seat. On finding none, she got busy reading the messages on her cell phone. Then suddenly she turned pale and dizzy; the phone fell from her hand. Somebody got up and gave her a seat. Arun's attention had been drawn to the thud of the cell phone on the floor and in no time, having requested a fellow passenger for some water, he was at Sarah's side. He made Sarah drink the water and gave her some sugar candy.

He waited for her to recover a bit. Then keeping aside his ethics, without any hesitation, he took the phone to read the message that had caused her to lose her balance.

The message was from her dad. "Enough of your nonsense! I have tolerated too much. Come back immediately on the next flight or be prepared to cut off from me forever."

He kept quiet, understanding the gravity of the situation. He helped her out of the bus, and remained with her silently, ensuring that she gathered her backpack correctly on the trolley from the conveyor belt.

"Can you please wait for me?" She stopped at an ATM machine on her way to the exit.

“Carry on. I will look after your luggage.” Arun assured her.

Without batting an eyelid, she rushed to the ATM, while Arun waited for her, watching her operate the machine.

He saw her struggling with her card and then read the instructions on the screen.

Her bank balance was showing as zero. She gave a command to collect the statement. She checked the statement and all at once lost consciousness. This last straw seemed to have broken her back completely.

Arun helped her away from the ATM, took out a bottle of water from her bag and splashed some water on her face.

As he quickly went through the statement which fell out of her hand, he realized that a huge sum had been withdrawn by someone today itself, leaving practically nothing in her account. “Sarah, everything is going to be alright. We will find a way out.” “How?” she asked in a lame voice. “I don’t want to go back to him.” “Why? He is your father, and he wants to have you back. What’s wrong?”

“It is not that simple. I will tell you some other time.”

Arun thought it unwise to quiz her any further. Instead, he arranged for a taxi, got her luggage loaded and then guided her to the back seat, while he sat in the front seat, next to the cab driver, periodically glancing behind out of concern.

She was completely lost as the taxi was moving through the busy streets of Mumbai. Even the few gestures of Arun to guide the taxi driver to the correct address did not bring her out of her stupor.

The taxi stopped outside the porch of a high-rise building. He held her hand and guided her to the lift.

Arun was quite surprised at the warmth that he was displaying by holding her firmly by her shoulders. Probably he was responding to her need for reassurance.

This is a crazy situation, thought Sarah. In the morning I get robbed by a stranger, in the afternoon I start getting close to a person whom I have never met before, and in the evening, I get disillusioned by the one person who I thought cared for me the most. And here I am, in some stranger's company, in some strange place, not even asking him where he is taking me or what he is planning to do with me.

The limp body in Arun's arms started stiffening slowly. By now she was aware about Arun's ability to do great guess work.

"I am better now. Thank you so much for taking care of me. You are a godsend for me."

"I am not."

"What?"

"I am doing it because as hard as I may try, my conditioning about the chivalrous nature of men will not permit me to leave a woman alone in times of distress. But as far as you are concerned, I have a feeling you would have handled yourself much better had I not been around. In fact, by now you would have called your dad to surrender to him and taken help from him."

When you help someone, make sure you are strengthening and not weakening the person in need of your help.

"I hate him. Don't talk to me about him." "Sorry!" said Arun.

"For a change you are sorry." Sarah had a mischievous look in her eyes.

Both of them had a hearty laugh.

Laughter is a great way to ease out the pains of life.

Laughing makes you breathe completely and fully. All of us have forgotten how to breathe. We seldom fill up our lungs to their full capacity to breathe out distress. Though it is a very natural gift, it remains underutilized and merely gets used as a survival aid rather than as an evolutionary mechanism.

Chapter One

"Good morning, rather Good afternoon." Sarah saw Arun entering the guest room with her eyes half open. It took her a while to realize that she was in Arun's house. He was formally dressed in a pearl white, long sleeved shirt. He appeared to be in a hurry to go somewhere.

"How are you feeling?" asked Arun, placing a mug full of hot black coffee on the side table. Without waiting for her response, he drew the curtains aside and opened the window of his apartment which overlooked Marine Drive. In front of her was a breathtaking view of the Arabian Sea reaching out to the horizon. Sarah had not even noticed the beauty of Arun's abode in the darkness last night.

"Good morning," Sarah replied as she attempted to spring up from her supine position. She was feeling embarrassed about oversleeping. "Sorry, I overslept. Did I hold you back from your work?" "Sorry again?" Arun stood like a giant pillar in front of her with his hands in his pockets ensuring that his facial expressions remained very serious.

"Oh no! Not again!" said Sarah breathing a deep sigh. "I can't help it, Arun, this is how I talk, you see!"

She chose to ignore his serious demeanor and tried to lighten his mood, as she got out of the bed and stood in front of him. With her fingers interlocked in front of her pubic bone, swaying her palms in an obviously awkward manner, she went a step closer to him and said, "You see, in America, good girls always use 'sorry', 'excuse me' and 'thank you'." Perhaps she was testing his patience. Her body language could have irritated any decent guy.

"And I guess I am a good girl. What do you say?" she looked straight into his eyes waiting for him to respond to her sex appeal. She wore a semi- transparent short slip with spaghetti straps and did not bother to wrap herself while getting out of the bed.

"Why do you need my approval?" Arun moved his eyes and body away from her, pretending to organize the room to its original tidy avatar.

"Arun! You are so serious all the time." She flung her hands in frustration. "Here I am making a joke to feel lighter, and you continue with your analysis. It becomes a bit too much at times!"

Quite often, without realizing it, some people use humor to escape the gloom. The greater the feeling of gloom and sadness, the more is the need for humor. And at times it seems out of place.

"Ok, Ok, I get it." He joined both his palms with the loud sound of a clap and raised them above his head, as his head bowed down to her slightly. Indians often use this kind of Namaste gesture to show that they give up. Before she could make any sense out of his baffling hand gesture, he extended both his palms to hold her shoulders as if to indicate that she needed to steady both her body and mind, because he was planning to tell her something extremely important.

"Listen Sarah," Sarah would have liked to distract him with some lighter conversation but the firmness of the touch of his palms on her bare shoulders and his serious demeanor prevented her from doing so. "Whether you like it or not, I need to talk some serious business with you... whenever you are ready for it... and this is about your future," said Arun, as he removed his car keys from the side pocket of his trousers. Surprisingly, he made no attempt to wait for her comment.

"I have kept a loaf of bread and some eggs in the fridge. I will organize some milk for you. Feel free to help yourself to whatever you want from the kitchen. I should be back in about three hours as there is some business to wind up. I was waiting for you to get up, so that I could speak to you before leaving the house."

"See you," he left in a hurry without waiting for any answer. He deliberately ignored Sarah's open mouth and extended right arm. Sarah felt as if she was begging for a few moments of his time to understand his next move.

Sarah would have felt insulted at this curt behavior by any other man. But she realized that she had no choice but to take it lying down. She was not sure if her father would be willing to take her back. Even if he did, his approach would be unpredictable. Any more grumbling and she might lose the last straw of hope that Arun represented, she thought, as she returned to bed to catch up on her sleep.

Intolerance is directly proportional to one's sense of power, and tolerance is directly proportional to the awareness of one's core strength. There is a difference between power and strength. Those who are aware of their inner strength do not care for power. Those who care for power could very well be compensating for a sense of inner weakness.

The doorbell rang and Sarah knew this was Arun. Quite a punctual guy, she thought.

"Hi! I am sorry I left in a hurry this morning! I had kept somebody waiting and that's why I had to rush."

Sarah was in no mood to greet him or comment on his 'sorry''.

She kept staring at him with a long face. She had a queasy feeling in her stomach because she sensed something serious was about to unfold.

He handed her a brown paper bag. "I got you a burger and some chips. I didn't know what you would have preferred for lunch. So, I played it safe. Hope you are okay with junk food."

Sarah simply nodded her head and set up the table for both. Arun was amazed at her movement in his house. The ease with which she moved did not match the status of an unknown refugee guest who had visited this place for the first time. She seems to have acquainted herself well...at least the kitchen part of it. He marveled, observing her every action.

Having lived all alone for many years, he had almost forgotten what it felt like to have a woman's presence in the house. All this while he had been very content just being by himself, with his all-round help, Ramu Chacha.

He liked the gentleness of Sarah's presence but chose to maintain his so-called 'serious sanity'.

What if this is a short-term experience? Of course, this is a short-term experience, he convinced himself.

It's pointless getting attached or repulsed by any experience because all experiences are transient in nature.

"Sarah, I have a farmhouse on the outskirts of Mumbai. That's where I grow my organic vegetables and fruits. In fact, I stay there most of the time and I have a visit due. Would you like to join me?"

"Oh! That's a fantastic idea! When do we return? I mean, I think I need to know this, so that I can carry my stuff accordingly."

"That depends on you. But definitely an overnight stay because it's quite tedious to drive back at night." As he stood with both his hands in his pockets, she felt a kind of eerie suspicion.

"Further discussion can be done at the farmhouse." When he talked, he seldom waited to assess her response.

I wish he had not said that again. Sarah felt her stomach churn and throat go dry, as she looked away towards the vast ocean through the large windows, in order to hide her disappointment.

Most of us are inherently intuitive. It's a different thing that some of us choose to consciously ignore these intuitive messages.

Finally, she took a deep breath, gathered her courage and turned to face him. "Arun, why don't we finish talking about whatever you want to talk about now, so that I can relax.

Honestly, this uncertain situation makes me feel queasy." Her eyes were genuinely pleading.

"Really? Let's talk," he ushered her to sit down opposite him. "What!" She looked at him with disbelief.

"I need to know what you are planning now." He plopped onto a soft leather sofa.

"I don't know. One thing is sure, I don't want to go back home until I find my guru. In fact, this evening I want to attend a short discourse by Swami Atmanandji. He seems to be very good. The problem is he speaks in Hindi and now I don't have money to hire a translator."

"Are you asking me to do this job free of cost?" The hard-hitting, sarcastic comment from Arun failed to discourage her.

Although she refrained from saying a single word, her facial expression and pleading eyes said it all.

"Sarah, your 'poor me' attitude might have helped you get away with many things in the past, but it's not going to work with me! So please stop playing that 'poor me'. Get out of it. You are no longer a small baby. Wake up to reality."

Sometimes words hit you harder than any other weapon.

"If you keep portraying this 'poor me' image to the world, you will only attract those who want to take advantage of you and make you feel more of the 'poor me'."

This was not the first time Sarah had been subjected to his curt behavior, but his body language, coupled with his cold and merciless statements, left her completely stunned. She had suddenly lost the capacity to react or think rationally. Then, before she could gather herself, she received the final punch.

"And yes, please keep me out of your games."

Sarah helplessly stared at him wide-eyed. After a few moments, when she managed to ease her tightened jaw muscles, she could only murmur sheepishly. "Are you planning to push me out of your house?"

"No. I am offering you a job at my farmhouse. Take it or leave it. There are plenty of people, many hungry men who will buy your 'poor me'!" Arun's voice was unusually stern and firm to the point of rudeness.

Sarah was stunned. Nobody had talked to her like this. What could she do? She was still feeling 'poor me' because of his behavior, but she did not dare say this to him. Would he ask her to move out of his house?

I can't understand him. Sometimes he is so nice and caring and on other occasions he hides this aspect of himself and behaves so ruthlessly.

"W..w..what kind of job?" she stammered as she asked him the question. "The job of a gardener. All you have to do is plant seeds and saplings, water them regularly and ensure that there are no weeds." Arun continued to remain firm, but his facial expression softened a bit with compassion.

"What will happen to my spiritual journey?"

"Well, you will have to decide between your survival and spiritual growth.

Decide right now."

"Can I give you the answer after meeting Swamiji? I have an appointment with him." Sarah was almost trembling with fear.

"I am leaving the house in the next 15 minutes. You have a choice of either coming with me or going for your meeting. Sarah, ***life is all about choices! Your future is shaped by the choices you make in the 'now'***" said Arun, leaving her alone on the sofa to contemplate and make up her mind.

Who would know that better than me? thought Sarah, as Arun called Ramu Chacha to help him lock up his flat.

The serene environment of Arun's house was intermittently stirred up by the hustle and bustle of winding up and packing. As she closed her eyes her entire life flashed in front of her. All the choices that she had made, had led her to rough stony roads, mountainous blocks, and dead ends...

Why? Why did I do all this? Can somebody explain this to me? What if I now get stuck in a survival rut? I had better go back to my dad and kneel in front of him. This guy Arun seems to be unpredictable.

"All right then, here I go." With a heavy heart she picked up her backpack and stood outside, waiting for the elevator door to open. Arun was still busy locking up the house. She silently went down to the building compound and started walking on the road.

Stepping out on the street she realized that she was absolutely clueless about her future. She didn't even have money to hire a cab. She considered selling her cell phone to generate some cash, but if she did that, she would lose the only means through which her dad could contact her. She had hoped that, as usual, her dad would reconcile and call her back. But he hadn't done it yet!

The phone vibrated. She felt relieved and excited at the same time.

Hope is a divine virtue, but not when it is used to compensate for one's own sense of shortcomings.

With a sense of optimism, she read the text from Joanna, her childhood friend and neighbor.

She turned pale again. She could not handle any more stress. She needed to sit somewhere and think of where to go. What now? Joanna had sent a note to congratulate her on her father's second marriage.

Oh! He actually got married again? He didn't even bother to inform me! Now I know why he was so eager to throw me out of his life. No wonder he appeared to have changed so much.

As her train of thought kept speeding up, she found herself breathing harder. When she dialed her father's cell number, a female voice answered. Perplexed, not knowing what to say, she quickly disconnected. The pink cheeks turned red, her eyes became moist, and her breathing turned rapid, all tell-tale signs of a severe emotional breakdown. She could have burst out with loud sobs on the sidewalk, but her mind got distracted as a silver-grey car stopped slightly ahead of her with the screeching sound of a very powerful brake.

Before she could think anything further, she saw the car reverse and halt right next to her. She turned her head ever so slowly, still almost thoughtless. The dark car window rolled down. She reckoned that it was Arun in the driver's seat, wearing brown sunglasses. But beyond that she drew a blank.

It took her another few seconds to come back to her senses. It seemed as if blinking hard was helping her get in touch with the present moment. She struggled to sound coherent as she could not bear to see Arun staring angrily at her.

"It's good you stopped," she whispered, still appearing slightly lost, trying hard to be in the 'now'.

"I left without saying thank you...uh., sorry.... I was in my own thoughts... thank you...um., for everything......." Her eyes had a genuine expression of gratitude, but her voice was barely audible.

Ignoring Sarah's 'thank you', Arun lashed out. "Though I don't like giving anyone anything for free, could I give you a piece of advice?" Without waiting for her consent, he continued, "The way you are standing on the roadside, you look like a whore. Get going, go home or go to your guru, unless you want to take this on as your career."

She was astounded. How could anybody be so heartless? The old Sarah would have been flustered at such a comment.

Well, I am not going to show my sorry side to him. She looked determined, with her moist eyes on the verge of flooding. "Is the job offer still open?" She started gathering herself emotionally as per the need of the situation.

Threatened survival manages to bring to surface a very different personality, perhaps the real one.

"Sure. What will you do?"

"I will do whatever you tell me to do." Arun was surprised. He failed to fathom what could have changed in such a short time.

If you don't walk on the path you are meant to walk on, the universe often sends signals by closing down the remaining pathways.

That's how we are all guided to walk on the path leading to our highest possible potential.

Sarah returned late in the evening with muddy hands and soiled shoes, appearing exhausted. Physical work is a very effective remedy for insomnia. She felt thoroughly drained and was drop-dead tired as she lay on the bed in the corner of the hut that Arun had provided in the servants' quarters of the farmhouse. Here, she lived with other fieldworkers and ate their kind of food. She kept her backpack in another corner and dried her clothes by hanging them on a line above her head. An ancient noisy fan comforted her during the hot summer nights and simultaneously helped her dry her clothes. For bathing and washing, she had a facility outside her hut. She did not bother to cook like the other co-workers but managed to eat whatever was served to all farmhouse workers.

Sarah found her fair skin gave her a definite advantage. Since she never threw her weight around (not that there was much left of it in any case) the women from the neighbourhood adored her for her complexion, beauty and simplicity. They would offer her their festive goodies as a mark of respect and care. The tradition of hospitality is truly alive in rural India. Indian culture requires the host to treat a guest as one would treat a deity. "Atithi Devo Bhava" was a term she had heard several times since her arrival in India; she was now experiencing it. The co-workers took great care of her. In fact, some of the women were a little upset with Arun for putting Sarah on a harsh job like farming.

Like all co-workers, she too had to pass through the veranda of Arun's farmhouse every morning. She had gotten used to seeing him pretending to read his morning newspaper. All farmhouse workers greeted him with respect while going to the fields and so did Sarah. Apart from his special effort to spend some time with Sarah to chat on some serious subject during his daily visit to the fields, he appeared to treat Sarah like any other farmhouse worker. To many of them, it was obvious that he kept an eye on her without her knowledge. He knew about her work attitude and preferences, he knew about her food and eating habits. That's why when Sarah started skipping meals at night out of sheer exhaustion, the news reached him soon.

The next morning when Sarah greeted him before going to the farm, he called out to her. "Sarah, come here." He was sitting on a lounge chair as usual, reading his newspaper. His juice and breakfast were served on the side table.

"Have a seat, Sarah." With his right hand pointing towards an empty cane chair next to him, he firmly indicated that she needed to sit there. He called Ramu Chacha, his Man-Friday and ordered scrambled eggs for her.

She politely refused. "Farmhouse workers in this estate don't have this kind of breakfast. Thank you very much, for offering though."

"Sarah, are you unhappy?" His voice was soft and he portrayed genuine concern.

"No, not exactly unhappy, but I am trying to adjust to this job. You see, when I was in America, I never had a 'job' as such. I think my father should have taught me some discipline." She was determined not to show her 'poor me' attitude.

"It is never too late, Sarah. But tell me, are you enjoying your job?"

"Yes," that was a loud and firm yes from her.

We spend so much energy trying to display exactly the opposite of what we feel from within.

Ask those people who try very hard by joking, laughing and making others laugh in order to mask their deepest grief and sorrows. Ask those who try very hard to portray how brave they are.

Probably they are masking the exact feeling that they are uncomfortable with.

"You are wrong. You are not enjoying it 100%, otherwise you wouldn't be so tired at the end of the day."

She looked down. She did not argue. Arun was no longer a co-passenger in the aircraft. Now he was the boss and she must show obedience to retain the job that she needed very badly right now.

The ecstasy of doing what you genuinely enjoy is the true elixir of life.

"Today, when you go to the farms, look around, try talking to the flowers, and taste some guavas from the tree. Drink water from the well, feel the soil in your hands." She looked baffled. "Listen to the music of blowing winds and the chirping of the birds," he continued. Remove your boots when you go to the farm today. Just feel connected to this land and tell me the difference in the evening."

Enjoying this farmhouse job? She tried to gauge her feelings about Arun's suggestion. Maybe it is possible.

Sarah was hesitant to take his advice because she was scared that if she really started liking this job, she would get stuck in this farmhouse forever.

Ironically, the lame fear of getting stuck in a situation keeps us away from enjoying the flow of life, and when we do not flow, we feel stuck in any case.

On the other hand, she did want to enjoy her work. Had her circumstances been any different, she definitely would have not chosen to be here in this condition. Since she was already stuck, there was no harm in trying it out, she chaffed. "Try not to look at your job merely as a survival mechanism; look at it as an experience of life, merely an amazing experience," Arun was saying.

Sarah simply nodded her head. Then gathering her wits, she spoke cautiously, "In the western world they say that when you can't avoid being raped, you might as well spread your legs and enjoy it."

Immediately, he sat upright in his lounge chair and regained his serious and stern posture. He realized that most of the farmhouse workers had left for work. "You may go now. Others must be waiting for you."

Today, she was given the job of plucking semi-ripe mangoes. She was given a special basket with a mouth as wide as a basketball ring. The basket could be attached to her waist, so that she could climb the tree and collect the fruits in her basket. From the amused looks of her co-workers, she assumed that she was either very awkward or this was the first time a woman was doing this job. She chose to ignore what they thought and simply focused on collecting mangoes. In between, she paused to eat some raw mangoes and she thoroughly relished them. She had been given a target to collect at least 50 mangoes and she felt a childlike thrill about this newfound adventure. She snatched some moments in between work to observe and smell the flowers. She even enjoyed the movement of earthworms in the muddy soil. In fact, she played with some of them with great fascination. To her amazement, she started becoming aware of not only the butterflies, but also of the many vibrant colors on their wings, something which she had been oblivious of until this moment.

During the lunch break, she ate the dry 'roti' with onion and chillies, like all other farmhouse workers, sitting cross-legged on the muddy soil without worrying about soiling her clothes. She found herself in a deep philosophical mood. *How silly of me to have ignored this beauty in nature.*

This must be happening to so many people, she thought. ***Rather than making the most out of the small little pleasures in life, people waste a lifetime waiting for their lives to shape up the way they think right.***

She took a deep breath to smell the fresh air and realized that she had not taken a lung filling breath for a long time.

There is so much fun in being able to breathe freely.

When she returned, she was almost dancing. She ate heartily that night and slept like a log.

As she was striding rapidly towards the farms the next morning, she saw Arun and rather than simply greeting him from a distance she spontaneously turned towards him. “Thank you so much, you made my day! I had great fun at the farm yesterday!” She made no attempt to contain her excitement. “Can I do the same job today?”

“You will have to find out from the supervisor. As far as I have heard, you overshot your target yesterday and did double compared to what was expected of you.”

Before Arun could complete his sentence, she was already running to the fields. Then she stopped and turned back towards him. “It has been a long time since I have hugged someone. May I give you a hug?”

Arun got up from his chair to give her a customary hug like he would have given to any female colleague, but to his great surprise Sarah ran towards him and clung to him like a baby chimp. And very spontaneously, she kissed him on his cheeks.

“I love you. And I mean it.” She looked at him hoping to get some positive response.

“I know. I can feel it.”

Sarah, like a good student of life, thought ***“It is not necessary to feel let down just because someone’s response does not match my expectations.”*** “Thanks. Thank you so much. You have touched me somewhere,” she gushed with heartfelt gratitude as he kissed her forehead.

As Sarah was returning to the farms, her thoughts took a different direction.

Is he gay? I haven't seen or heard about any woman in his life. In the West, any straight man with a woman in desperate need of help, would have asked her to offer her services in his bed, instead of at his farms and fields.

It had been a long time since she'd had great sex! Sarah realized that her mind had gone off track and she forced herself to get back to the 'moment'. It is easy to focus on 'don't haves' rather than on 'haves', she argued with herself.

It is interesting how the human mind keeps focusing on the 'lack' rather than the 'stack', even though most of the time, the quality and quantity of the stack is much more than what we lack.

Gains and drains of life are absolutely relative. What appears to be a gain could be the result of a drain. What appears to be a drain is a precursor to gain. It's one's choice to focus on the gain or the drain.

Peace is the product of prudent preferences made at the level of prime presence.

She quickly diverted her mind from the topic and started focusing on her work once again. Today's job was quite mundane though. She had to simply collect the weeds and put them in cane baskets. She was surprised how easily she could do it. Her body did not hurt despite bending down repeatedly with the cane basket.

Post lunch she saw Arun coming towards the fields. She was wondering why she was feeling so happy to see him today. After giving some routine instructions to the farm supervisor, when

Arun turned towards Sarah, she noticed a mild acceleration in her heartbeat.

"Hi! How is the work going on?" He asked, standing opposite her with his hands in his pockets as usual.

"Fine, I am enjoying it," she smiled and lifted her shoulders slightly in agreement.

He bent down and picked up some soil in his cupped palms.

"The soil has the potential to give you all that you were looking out for in those Ashrams."

"How?" she asked, quite bewildered.

"When you work with your heart and soul, you will realize that there are very few thoughts that bother you. You feel so much in harmony and peace with yourself... But the experience could very well be the opposite, if you tend to punish yourself by hating your work."

Something stirred inside. She continued listening to him spell bound.

Were these the words her soul craved to listen to?

"You will feel very connected with the entire universe. Even though you are miles away from your roots, working on these unknown farms, you will feel completely connected and rooted."

He had said it! How does he know exactly what I want to say? In fact, he gives better expression to my thoughts. Sarah could not stop feeling amazed. "Is this something called Karma Yoga?" She looked at him with childlike curiosity. Immediately after uttering these words, she became slightly tense. *What if he got irritated with the subject again?*

"What is Yoga, Sarah?" The child in her felt relieved as Arun actually continued the conversation which meant a lot to her.

"Well, I know some aspects of Yoga, a few Asanas and Pranayama. Rishi Patanjali has described the eight-fold path of...."

"My question is very simple. What is Yoga?" intervened Arun.

"***Yoga means a union... union with the Divine, union with the Creator***," Arun continued without waiting for Sarah to give him the relevant answers. In any case, Arun rarely asked questions to get answers from others.

Interestingly he chooses to ask questions, so that others open up to get their own answers.

"When you do what you are supposed to be doing, you feel one with the Creator. That is Yoga. You do not have to learn Yoga from books or do rigorous training. Yoga is in the mind. To attain union, you have to shed the barrier. The Divine is seeking this union with you as much as you are."

"The barriers that we have created around us are not letting us reach out to the Divine and those are the barriers of ignorance. Most people think that God lives somewhere in heaven and we need to reach out to Him. In fact, it is the other way round, the Divine is in everything that we see, feel, touch, smell or taste. The Divine is something that our senses cannot perceive. The Divine is ever eager to get in touch with us and communicate with us. Did you ever feel one with the Creator while working in this field? If not, pursue it and you will experience this oneness."

Overwhelmed, Sarah fell at his feet. "You are the guru that I was looking for. Make me your disciple! Please?"

"Sorry!" Arun stepped back and walked away.

Sarah's heart sank as she saw through the veil of tears, her messiah fading away like a mirage.

Oh no! Why is life so difficult? It takes me ages to find a guru and when I find one, he simply rejects me. He walks away without explaining his refusal. Why? I don't understand him. How do I handle this? At times he simply fascinates me and at times he spooks me. One day he gives me hope and on another he disappoints me.

For the next few days Arun was nowhere to be seen. She inquired with the farm supervisor and found out that he was in Mumbai for some business work.

She kept waiting to see him. He had left her feeling so incomplete.

However, she started working on his guidelines. She started being in the 'now'. She started experiencing a state of calmness and peace almost all the time.

Running away from home was now a thing of the past, a thought which she no longer wanted to dwell on. She did not bother to call her father. The calling card on her cell phone had run out of its validity period, but she had no desire to get it renewed.

She had basically no desire to remain in touch with the world that she had left behind.

She hadn't even checked her email, something that was inconceivable a few days ago.

She started taking each day at a time. She no longer hoped to see Arun back at the farmhouse. She developed a kind of a faith that each coming day was definitely going to be better than the rest. ***Instead of deciding what is supposed to be the best for me, it is prudent to make the best out of every moment of my life***, she thought to herself. ***When you pre-decide what is good for you, and keep waiting for that to happen, you miss out on the opportunities to experience the goodness of the existing moments.***

Though she missed Arun, she knew that she could not control him in any way. She had no right to do so. All that she could do was to handle herself effectively. She guessed that this is what Arun often referred to as 'emotional independence'.

Emotional Independence! How much he cherishes his independence. If he was so independent, he would have handled my request that he be my guru in a much better way. Anyway, who am I to judge him? Why, after all, should I judge him? She kicked a tiny pebble, walking on a stony pathway of the farm, lost in thought.

She found this activity quite interesting. *Let me see if I can kick the next one still farther away.* She kicked the next one with even more force. Hey! *This is fun, even the pebbles on a stony path can delight me! She almost felt like a small kid. I've discovered a great new game on this plain land. Now, I can play this game every day.*

The five-year-old kid, who would go bird watching with her mother and her mother's new boyfriend, emerged in her.

This five-year-old Sarah took over the adult personality as she drifted back to her childhood days. It used to be so much fun to go out with them. Uncle Tim, as she called him, used to buy her ice cream, chocolates and gifts every time they met.

Suddenly she jerked her head as she remembered Arun telling her to be in the now. So many gurus and philosophers around the world had been talking mystically about being in the now and in the moment, but it was only being at the farmhouse that she was experiencing this on a consistent basis. Directly and indirectly, Arun helped her remain in the present.

She mentally thanked Arun while kicking one more pebble, and guess who was at the receiving end?

Arun had been watching her as she strolled closer to the farmhouse. "Hi!" He said, ignoring the hit of the pebble. "Hi! How are you? When did you arrive? How was your trip?" Sarah made no attempt to contain her overwhelming excitement. "Too many questions! Tell me what it is that you really want to know." Sarah blushed. None of the answers really mattered to her.

Genuine communication often gets masked behind vain 'attempts at verbalization'.

"Nothing, you are right as usual. I wanted to know nothing, honestly. Of course, you must have arrived after I left for the farm." She looked down preparing to open up her heart.

"I just wanted to say thank you." She looked up, relieved that Arun was still there listening to her patiently. She felt encouraged to go on. "I am enjoying myself on this farm. It is bright, sunny, with lots of fresh air and plenty of peace. I don't dwell on my past as much as I used to and I haven't been worrying about the future either."

Arun was patiently listening to her. For a change, his hands were not in his pockets as he stood facing her.

"I have been taken care of in the past, so there is no reason why I would not be taken care of in the future too." Sarah's eyes moistened with tears of joy and gratitude.

"Thank you," she almost choked.

Arun was at a loss for words so he gently broke the spell with subtle warmth and asked, "How about joining me for dinner tonight?"

"Yeah, sure. What time? Where?" she said as she checked her tears with her index finger.

"At 8, in the dining room of the farmhouse."

"Done! I will be there. Thank you so much." *This will also give me a chance to learn a few more things from him.*

The excitement in her voice was obvious, though she tried controlling her overtly expressive behaviour out of the fear of being judged by him. Besides, she did not want a repetition of the former experience of him walking away after she had tried touching his feet.

Eight o'clock was two long hours away from now. Almost one hundred and twenty minutes, seven thousand two hundred seconds... She borrowed a mirror from her neighbor, took a good hot water bath, and fetched her black semi formal gown with a boat shaped neckline and generously sprayed herself with the perfume which had sunk very deep in her backpack. Hmm, a date with a difference! By choosing to take his advice of being in the present and knowing Arun's unpredictability, she stopped imagining what was going to happen over dinner. She completely prepared herself to be surprised.

The pleasantness or unpleasantness of an outcome is decided by the attached expectations.

The dining table of this house was very rustic in nature, with dinner mats made of straw and all the cutlery was from the local market.

A beautiful lamp was lit at the center of the table. The soft yet hypnotically rhythmic melody of a tabla and santoor recital was bringing a new life to the otherwise silent and still environment. She sniffed a little deeper to guess the fragrance of the incense he had used. It felt as serene as a temple.

The serving bowl contained creamy mushroom soup and garlic bread. She saw penne in a tomato sauce dusted with dried oregano.

"Wow!"

It had been ages since she had relished good Italian food. *How did he know about my taste and preference? I have never spoken to him about it. The local food cooked for servants, though always tasty, especially 'Daal Chaval', was getting monotonous. Oh! how my taste buds craved for something different.*

"You were craving for this kind of food, weren't you?" Arun entered the room and ushered her to take a seat opposite him at the dining table.

She blushed. “Actually, yes! I am grateful for the food until now that has helped me survive, though lately I have been losing interest.” Arun stared at her with a serious look. But before he could open his mouth to drop another bombshell, she quickly intervened, “Please don’t lecture me anymore. I really want to enjoy the food tonight.”

“Sure, go ahead.” The host in him chose to let his guest enjoy her food. The heady combination of ethereal ambience and a handsome companion

...What more could she ask for?

“Thank you once again.” Sarah was glowing with happiness as she expressed her sincere gratitude to him.

“You are welcome.” His response to her gratitude left her elated enough to make her throw her hands up in the air and say, “Oh! My dear God, I am feeling so honored today.”

“There is nothing to feel honored about.” He could not have been more curt and cold in his conduct. “This is going to be a part of your job, tomorrow onwards.”

“What? My job? What kind of job? Eating dinner with you?”

“Yes, and much more.” He picked up a garlic crouton and passed it to her. “We will talk about it after dinner. Let’s enjoy dinner right now.”

“Oh! OK.”

Let me enjoy every bite...Who knows, this could be the last meal of my life. Sounds pessimistic, doesn’t it? Sarah thought in her mind as she took a bite of garlic bread. No, perhaps very optimistic....

If you want to live life to your fullest, always keep this most powerful thought in your mind, 'this day could be the last day of my life.'

She had not experienced the truth of this statement in her life when she had heard it from Arun earlier. However, since then, she had stopped cribbing about life as she was busy surviving and making the most out of the opportunities that life brought her way.

"Amazing food!" She complimented her host. "After a long time!" she said, followed by a long sigh.

"Take a guess! There is a reason why this food tastes so great."

Sarah looked at him to assess his facial expression, before risking another blunder, "You made it?" Sarah had a child-like look of disbelief on her face.

"Who else do you think can cook Italian around here?" She was seeing glimpses of different aspects of Arun's personality.

As they finished their dinner, he instructed Ramu Chacha to serve the dessert from the fridge. Sarah stared at the Tiramisu being served at the table.

"Did you make this too?" She laughed.

"No, though I was tempted to lie in order to impress you further, let me be honest and tell you that I got this for us from Mumbai."

Oh my God! He took it for granted that I would say yes to his invitation for dinner. The woman in her started feeling restless once again. *Why am I so predictable to him?*

"I am eager to listen to what you have to say about my next job." She wanted to now move on and escape before her thoughts and feelings became more transparent to Arun and made her feel any more vulnerable.

"Finish your dessert and then we'll talk in the garden."

Sarah had trained her mind to be in the 'now' and it was turning out to be of great help in testing moments like this. Her attention now turned to sensing how the cool creamy dessert was diluting the acidic feeling in her stomach.

"Tell me Sarah, how is life treating you here?" "This life is helping me survive." "And how are you treating your life over here?"

How life treats you depends upon how you treat your life.

"I am taking each breath as if it was the last. You taught me to do that." Both of them continued to stroll gently under the star-studded sky.

"Do you know Sarah, I don't read a lot, but my greatest learning is from a very special school."

Sarah stopped as she wanted to know which school had taught him so much. "Which school, Arun?"

"The name of that school is LIFE."

Oh, I know he is witty but his wit has so much wisdom. He is so right. What life has taught me in the last few weeks, no guru has been able to teach me in the last several months. She would have gone on a journey back in time had she not been interrupted by Arun's voice.

"No school on Earth can teach us, as much as this school called LIFE!"

"So, what did you learn from your life, Sarah?" He suddenly stopped walking and turned towards her. This compelled her to face him.

"Until I came here to this farm, my life had offered me a lot of learning but there was no one in my life to guide me to extract its essence. Even if the lessons came along in a natural way, I tried to run away or reacted to them unnecessarily or just escaped. That's what I did when I came down to India."

"Oh! So, you realize your visit to India was a superb escape drama and not a spiritual search of any kind."

"But it was a spiritual search, only my intention behind it was more to escape than spiritual growth. In fact, very often I find myself questioning my fundamental beliefs about spirituality. If spirituality is the feeling of being one with God, I did experience it while working in the fields these past few days. The kind of feelings I have been through are difficult to describe, Arun."

"You don't have to, Sarah. I too have experienced what you are going through right now, and my journey still continues." Arun extended his palms almost involuntarily to hold Sarah's hands. "I have a lot to learn from life, Sarah. There is so much conditioning which I need to work upon. You see..." he stopped, as Sarah's fingers touched his lips disallowing him from completing his sentence.

"Please don't talk anymore about any of your weaknesses. I am too scared to lose the one man I see as God."

“God?” He laughed aloud. He was having a difficult time regaining his balance. His laughter almost turned devilish in the silence of the dark night. Finally, he managed to control himself. “Sarah, you remember I walked away when you tried touching my feet?” This bizarre behavior from an otherwise very serious person was creating a funny sensation in her stomach. “I moved away because I did not want to play your guru.”

“Why? In this short span you have taught me so much. Why am I being deprived of this privilege? Tell me what I need to do to deserve the status of your disciple?” Sarah was serious but Arun was not. He laughed aloud once again.

“Do you want me to disappear from your life forever?” “No”

“Then don’t even talk about this guru business - ever. Or else I might never see your face again.”

They spent the rest of the evening quietly listening to the sound of cicadas, looking at the star- studded sky and walking on the stony pathways of the farmhouse.

It is amazing how the same sky appears different in the city and different in rural areas. Do the stars like to shine more brightly for these noble hearted villagers? Or do the city guys offer strong competition against these naturally sparkling beings?

They took a big round of the farm using a battery-operated torch, before finally returning back to the house without uttering a single word.

“You were to talk to me about my next job profile, Arun.” Sarah broke the silence, when she realized that the night walk had come to an end and they were just a few feet away from the servants' residence area where she lived.

"You don't have to go to the fields from tomorrow. You will not have to report to the farm supervisor. You have done a great job and you are being promoted now to the next position. You may use the guest bedroom at the house as your accommodation, so pack up your stuff tonight and get ready to shift tomorrow."

But this information was not enough for Sarah, "What am I expected to do from tomorrow?"

Arun stopped walking. In the darkness of the night, he tried gazing into Sarah's inquisitive eyes. He moved a step closer to her and gently whispered with a slight grin on his otherwise serious face, "You are expected to please me."

Sarah's jaw dropped as she froze, she did not know what to think, or how to react.

"Good night." Arun kissed her on the forehead, and gave her a warm hug as he left her near the entrance of her cottage.

She simply stood there for several minutes before the woman in her woke up and flooded her mind with several unspeakable, disturbing thoughts.

Why could he have not revealed this aspect of himself right in the beginning? I thought he was a safe kind of guy.

This kind of behaviour from men was not a new scenario in her life but this was the last thing she expected from Arun. She had put him on a very high pedestal and now she was afraid, afraid to face the possibility of her God having feet of clay.

She spent the whole night almost without blinking.

Her thoughts were not about losing her job, but about losing that image of her ideal man.

You always want to see people around you in a jacket, which you have designed as per your judgment and beliefs, based on your past experiences. Friction in relationships often results when others refuse to fit into the jacket you have created in your mind for them.

It has often been observed, "The *emotional, physical and social discomforts and dis-ease in general are the end - a culmination of acts of wearing ill-fitting and inappropriate robes chosen by you and others.*"

Chapter Two

The next day Arun entered Sarah's cottage at 9 am on the dot. Most of the farmhouse workers had just left for work. A few children and women folk were still in the neighboring huts. Sarah was sitting on a traditional wooden cot which had a cotton strap mesh as a base. Her head was drooping down and she had left the entrance door wide open. Clothes hanging on the rope had been neatly packed up in the backpack.

Arun stood at the entrance with his left hand in his pocket and with his right index finger playfully gyrating the car keys. "Tell me where I should ask Ramu Chacha to shift this luggage? To the guest room or the car?"

She raised her head with an indignant, angry look. *He knew that I was thinking of quitting.* She lost all control. Impulsively picking up an empty clay vase lying next to her, she threw it in his direction. Arun ducked with a sheepish grin, making her even angrier.

Anger is the result of a deep sense of helplessness. Sadness is the end result of helplessness generated by unattended anger.

"You know about it!... Why do you play these games with me? You know exactly how I am feeling." She paused to take a very deep breath. "You...bloody heartless fellow... Get out of here, just get lost!" Her voice was hoarse with anger. Her entire body trembled.

Living in India had "Indianized" her to a great extent. She had adapted herself to the extent that she had even begun to speak with an Indian accent most of the time. But in rage, the old, American Sarah, who never completed a single sentence without some of her favorite expletives, surfaced. And that didn't surprise Arun at all....

Arun turned towards the main entrance to leave her to calm down on her own. Just as he reached the entrance, he heard loud sobs which compelled him to turn. Neighbors rushed towards her cottage to find out if it was anything serious.

"Come to my office to collect your payment before the driver drops you to the city," Arun said firmly, as he walked out and gestured to the others to leave her alone.

Sarah was down with a very high fever throughout the day. She felt extremely weak. She had no energy to walk up to his cabin. She probably did not want to face him alone. Her peace of mind had vanished. The practice of being in the now was a story of the past.

Why do I always attract men like my father, where I have to please them for my survival? I don't want to do it anymore! But if I don't do it, where do I go now? I don't think I can get employment so easily. No chance. What about my spiritual journey? Does it end here? She kept thinking aloud. How can I comply with him like this? She kept grumbling in her mind all throughout the day.

Our mind is like a cluttered cupboard where negative thoughts are dumped together randomly. Pull out one and many more

will tumble out. If you have one negative thought in your mind, surely many more will follow immediately.

For two days she had a very high fever but Arun did not go to see her. Instead, he called for a physician to treat her. Gangubai and the neighboring women remained by her side, nourishing her with rice soup. In the Western and Southern parts of India, rice soup and coconut water are considered to be a great remedial measure during sickness.

These random little acts of kindness without any need for reciprocation are a hallmark of our evolution as humans.

In sheer agony, Sarah was overwhelmed and genuinely touched by this angelic expression of unconditional love and care coming from complete strangers. She wondered if this was God's way of soothing the pain she had suffered at the hands of Arun's ruthlessness. The seeker in Sarah translated this as God's way of communicating to her that she was taken care of.

We are taken care of at all times. The question is whether we recognize, appreciate and allow that care.

She gathered all her courage and went to his bedroom located on the mezzanine floor of his farm house. He had kept his door wide open as if he was expecting her to walk in at any moment.

Did he sense my arrival? She wondered.

He looked up and saw her approaching but continued with the magazine that he was reading. She went to him, took the magazine from his hands and sat on the armrest of his sofa, leaning on him while putting both her arms around his neck. She was about to kiss him on his lips, when he said, "Sarah, can you please sit there?" Arun maintained a very polite tone as he requested her to sit on a sofa opposite him. Sarah stared at him aghast. Her cheeks turned red with embarrassment. A part of her wanted to run away... far, far away...

Nothing crushes the ego more than rejection and people take a long time to recover from it.

Her experience with men had taught her that it was she who had the prerogative to reject men. Each time she rejected a man, she got a kind of kick out of it. But she had not been at the receiving end so far.

What's wrong? Is he celibate or is he gay? He can't be gay! He doesn't give out that kind of vibe. So, what went wrong? She took a quick sniff to check out if she smelled awful. Perhaps, her breath smelled foul because of her recent illness.

Before she could analyze further, Arun spoke through the silence. "I think you misunderstood when I told you that your job is to please me." Sarah felt cold and stiff. A strange kind of shiver ran up her entire spine,which made her sit upright. Her eyes did not leave Arun's face. Arun got up from the sofa and started gently pacing up and down the room, as if he was about to make a great philosophical statement.

"Suppose I had given you the job of pleasing an old gentleman suffering from paralysis. How would you have handled the situation?" Arun stopped pacing and leaned towards her, resting his hands on the back rest of the sofa. "Think for a while."

Sarah took a few moments to regain her composure. Something in her started feeling silly and yet safe as Arun put forward his question.

"Hmm...I probably would find out what pleases him - his likes and dislikes. Maybe I would put some flowers in his room or change the curtains to more colorful ones; read him a book which is light and humorous; take care of his diet, and maybe even a massage on a regular basis might make him happy." Sarah almost whispered. She was beginning to understand his point but found it difficult to believe in the possibility.

"So............... you could think of all these ideas in the case of an old gentleman, but not in mine. Why?"

Arun added the last word emphatically slamming his left clenched fist into his right open palm.

"Because you're not old." She almost muttered. "But I am still a gentleman." He smiled with dignity. She blushed once again and sheepishly left the room.

He wants me to please him without really touching him. Now that's a challenge. He is right, the only way I know of pleasing men in my life is through sex. Even my father.........

Her estranged mother left a 10-year-old Sarah behind, under the care of her father, George, to search for happiness in her new marriage.

Since then, she found her best friend in her dad. Every night she would hug him and go to sleep. After the traumatic divorce, George did not find it sensible to get married again. Instead, he decided to focus on nurturing Sarah. His whole attention now turned to his little angel. Sarah was now the center of his universe. For this little girl, life was fun. The feeling of being needed by her dad was a deeply satisfying and fulfilling experience.

The need to be needed is directly proportional to insecurities in relationships. It is like an insurance policy to protect ourselves from the future possibility of rejection. All of us have a need to be needed. But those who have experienced rejection or emotional insecurity, may have a compulsion to be needed.

Sarah and her dad both had that need. She tried her best not to let her dad feel the absence of her mother. She tried handling the household chores. Every Sunday morning was spent cleaning up the house. Invariably they would have their lunch in a Mexican restaurant because she loved enchiladas. Later they would buy groceries for the house, set up the kitchen for the week, and settle down for a nice movie in the evening. She did not even realize when she crossed her 11th birthday.

One fine day she got up in the middle of the night feeling wet. She went to the bathroom and did not come out for a long time. When her father switched on the reading light next to the bed, he discovered the bed linen full of blood stains.

He called out to her, standing outside the bathroom. All he could hear in response were her loud sobs.

He pushed the door open to find her weeping in the corner with blood-stained clothes, crouched in a fetal position.

"I want my mom. Where is she? I want to go back to my mom. I need her." He tried to hug her but she would not allow that. She kept crying aloud. Her dad felt completely devastated. He had never regretted breaking away from Sarah's mom as much as he did that night. Though he had been expecting this day for a while, he just did not have the heart to discuss this matter with her. Silently, he walked across to the storage shelf and removed a pack of sanitary napkins that he had purchased for her a couple of months back. Then he took out one of her panties from the chest and carefully lined it with the napkin the way he had once seen her mom, Ami, do. As he handed over this piece of reassurance and security to her, he took a deep sigh of relief, "Wear this and come out. You will be ok."

As he prepared himself to go back to bed to catch up with his remaining sleep after changing the bed linen, he silently congratulated himself for not being jittery about handling this crucial day.

The next day, her father returned home with books on women's sexuality, which he silently handed over for her perusal.

With the recent changes in Sarah's life, things swiftly began to change between Sarah and her father, George. She was no longer an innocent little girl. She would not hug him anymore. She started becoming moody. She started throwing temper tantrums.

George began getting really scared of her mood swings and responses now. At times he did not know how to react. He felt more depressed with every passing day. He had lost his sweet little Sarah!

Gradually, the situation started easing out. She demanded a separate bedroom. She got one. She started maintaining a silent distance. She would sleep with her bedroom locked.

'Anything for you sweetheart', the doting father said in his mind.

Six months passed by and her skinny body started blossoming into one of a curvaceous woman. She started gaining a lot of weight. George helped her buy a suitable bra from a good store. That too embarrassed her. She kept complaining to her dad that the salesgirls were grinning at her.

On the eve of her 13th birthday, he bought a big teddy bear for her. Instead of gifting it to her in the conventional gift-wrapped format, he thought of giving her a surprise.

He wanted to quietly place this teddy next to her under the quilt. He prayed that she would forget to lock her room door that night. At 11:59 p.m., he tip-toed into her room thanking his stars that the door was unlocked. He went close to her bed with the big teddy in his hands to place it next to her under her quilt.

As he pulled the rug to do so, he froze. Sarah was sleeping stark naked. She woke up with a shock. The last thing she expected was for her dad to come inside and pick up the quilt like that. She felt awkward and embarrassed. Before she could open her mouth to say something, he quickly stepped out of the room, saying sorry.

For several nights after that, sleep eluded both of them.

For her father, Sarah reminded him of Ami, his first love. It had been years since he had been close to a woman. In an attempt to become a dedicated father, he had completely suppressed his sexual drive.

The naked body of his daughter had definitely triggered something in him. Even as he worked in his office, the vision of her nude form kept coming in front of his eyes. He felt guilty, he felt uneasy, and he felt perplexed. He could not comprehend it.

Am I feeling attracted to her? How can I? She is my daughter!

He had to argue with himself several times a day. Coming home to face her had become a big ordeal. Most of the time, he came home late. Sarah would leave his dinner on the dining table and go to sleep with her room locked. He rarely got up to say bye to Sarah as she left for school every day.

This confusion stayed with him regardless of his attempts to shake it off. Sarah, on the other hand, felt very dirty from within with that night's undue exposure. She cursed herself for not having locked her room that fateful night. Simultaneously, she was also experiencing a strange kind of pleasure. The birthday surprise for her, on a different level, gave her an unexpected excitement.

Eventually, Sarah learnt to handle herself. Slowly she started feeling settled in her approach. But her dad had to take several sessions with a counselor.

The situation at home changed concurrently. Sarah began to experience a strange thrill when George came home from the office. Her father too started looking forward to rushing home as early as possible. He started spending weekends at home rather than going for a game of golf.

It was when she crossed 14 that the duo went for a holiday to the Bahamas.

She spent three weekends searching for a nice bikini to wear during the trip.

It had been a long time since Sarah had enjoyed a good vacation apart from her customary school trips. She was full of excitement. She remembered all those precious moments she'd had as a child on holidays with her mom and dad.

When they reached their shack, the first thing she said was "Dad, are we sharing the bedroom?"

"Would you like to check into another shack? I can organize it." Dad tried hiding his disapproval. He had learnt the art of handling a teenager by now.

The best way in which you can deal with stubborn and adamant people is by not being stubborn and adamant with them.

"Leave it. I'll be fine. Anyway, it's too scary and lonely staying in an individual shack on this island hotel."

They had a great time bathing in the ocean and in the bright sunlight. Relaxed, they settled down in the bar. George had never sat with her like this in a bar. This was a special day in her life too and another milestone in their lives!

He watched her guzzle down her first peg of gin rapidly. Sarah had become tipsy on her very first peg. Yet she continued ordering one peg after the other. Her indulgent dad kept watching her getting drunk but did not make any serious effort to stop her from drinking further. With every drink, she felt as if she was freeing herself from her own inhibitory clutches. She started talking aloud. Her speech began to slur. It became difficult to sit there as she was almost slouching on the sofa. Finally, he had to carry her in his arms to their shack.

After putting her limp body in the bed, he kept watching her uninhibitedly for minutes together. He kept looking at her golden locks of hair scattered all over the pillow. He kept watching her body-hugging top making a futile attempt to hide her breasts, moving rhythmically with every breath. Her belly button was smiling at his conflict. He could not ignore her lovely long legs, which were practically fully exposed, as her tight leather skirt had risen up exposing her skimpy underpants. His body experienced thousands of sensations that night. His head was flooded with millions of thoughts. It took a while before he could come back to his senses.

He was exhausted by his vain attempts to remind himself that he was the father of this beautiful babe and not her boyfriend.

He spent the first part of the night engaging in a self-defeating debate with himself and attempting to numb himself with some more booze. Eventually he allowed his basal instinct to take over without worrying about the future consequences.

Alcohol is often used as an excuse to cover up all sorts of human weaknesses that we dare not admit and expose otherwise.

The morning brought with it realizations and possibilities of lame explanations justifying the previous night. To his utter surprise he had to explain nothing. The fact that she had not woken up in the same clothes that she had worn to the beach the night before, did not seem to bother Sarah.

She loved the vacation. She looked forward to getting drunk and the follow up act of intimacy with the masculine principle.

In spite of the tremendous conflict in his mind, he continued on his adventurous exploratory trips night after night. She continued to pretend to be drunk and before dawn set in, he would dress her up in her pajamas to avoid embarrassment and confrontation. In the morning both of them pretended to ignore the previous night's events.

It is not just alcohol but the overwhelming exuberance of teenage, which successfully helped her in benumbing the

After the vacation, Sarah shifted back into Dad's bedroom. She started behaving like a fully matured woman.

Both of them did not find the need for another partner.

This went on for quite some time. She began to exercise hard to shape up her slightly plump figure. She started looking more attractive with every passing day.

After money, sex is the second most important driving factor, in people's lives.

Soon Sarah entered university, and her outlook towards life changed completely. She stopped taking interest in household stuff. She started spending weekends with her friends in pubs. She had quite a few friends and she was particularly fond of one of them who she dated very often.

George did not know how to curb her and acted quite possessive at times. Sarah could not understand why he should be so insecure. She had the full right to lead a normal life.

She started spending her Sundays with boyfriends. Even after coming home, she was constantly busy talking on the phone or with her laptop on the internet. This made him feel very lonely and left out. The dad in him was happy in a way because it meant that Sarah was growing up like any other normal American teen, but without Sarah to indulge in, he felt purposeless.

He had made Sarah his world. He had no other relationship to look forward to. He had lost touch with most of his friends. He wondered whether he should have remarried earlier when Sarah was younger. He often contemplated why he had waited for her to grow up. Their relationship started becoming more and more strained as a part of him expected Sarah to spend some time with him.

Sarah, on the other hand, had multiple choices now, besides her father. She deduced that he did not like her dating other boys but chose to ignore his feelings and temper tantrums. In fact, she realized how important she had become in his life. Every gesture of hers really mattered to him. He cared for intimate moments with her. He craved for the joy he got when on rare occasions Sarah gave him her undivided attention. He would eagerly wait to hear her giggling at the dining table. When she sneaked inside his quilt and held him tight, he felt a tremendous sense of fulfillment. Every time they had sex, he felt secure about her.

At times people's hearts care more for emotional intimacy than physical. Perhaps George was one of them, but Sarah's immaturity prevented her from perceiving this. She started bartering her body for extra money and George helplessly complied.

Both of them did not like this. He had an emotional need for physical intimacy which she thoroughly exploited.

If you choose not to be exploited, choose not to be needy.

Later, her demand for money kept increasing and his need for sex started reducing. She could no longer extract the money the way she used to once upon a time.

"I am calling up Mom. You know why? Because you are not giving me the money. I will tell her that I am no longer sleeping with you so you're refusing to give me money."

He was devastated. He had never expected this sort of blackmail from her.

Eventually that blackmail ended with a kind of truce between the two of them. He assigned a fixed sum for her as pocket money and she agreed to ask for no more, while he reconciled to the fact that he had to leave her alone with boys of her age. He conceded that she was a grown up and needed him no more except for the money.

But there was more to come as she now started blackmailing both Ami and George, simultaneously.

Sarah started making George feel guilty for using her body.

She wouldn't miss out a single chance to remind him about it.

She started winning sympathy from her mother too for leaving her alone with her dad at such a tender age.

Her mother was going through her own break-up in her second marriage. Ami instigated Sarah to demand her own apartment, separate from her father.

He complied with her demand and got her a rented apartment. She spent two years by herself in this apartment, sleeping with a different man every night, demanding cash and kind from everyone she slept with.

Sarah started getting depressed. She realized that her father hardly called her now. They would meet once a month when she would go to collect her money.

As her father started getting disinterested in her and her lifestyle, she too started getting disinterested in the money, her body and all the things money could buy. She got plenty and she spent plenty but nothing made her feel good about herself.

She started feeling more and more sick from within. Her body started feeling used.

She did not want any man to touch her now. There was a deep emptiness for something which she could not fathom. Smoking was no longer comforting, so she tried various narcotic drugs and substances. But these too could not numb the void within. She started surfing the internet voraciously to look for the answer to what to do with herself.

When she moved in with her dad once again, George found her completely changed. She appeared listless. She slept for hours. She would not bother to eat for days and at other times she would binge.

Psychiatrists and psychotherapists could help her, but very little. She was losing interest in everything.

George started coming home late deliberately. Seeing her condition would make him feel more guilty and sorry for her. He had no heart to face her. He would come heavily drunk, late in the night and would go straight to bed.

It may seem strange, but in a relationship, ***when we cannot see our loved ones going through emotional or physical pain, subconsciously we avoid them. This attempt to escape only worsens the situation.***

George did exactly the same. He did not have the heart to face Sarah. One morning, she woke him up early. "I want to go to India," she announced, standing next to his bed.

"Why?" asked George, trying to recover from the surprise that his daughter had just thrown at him.

"I want to meet my guru. Only a guru will be able to help me in finding my answers," Sarah said.

"What guru? Which answers?"

"I tried surfing the net but I could not find the one. I think I will have to go personally and look out for one."

"Don't be naive! You sound as if a guru is a kind of commodity, you can shop for in an Indian market!" He had made no attempt to hide his disgust.

"Are you mad? "You are not going!" declared her mother, after listening to her decision. "The gurus will squeeze you out more than what your dad has. Forget about gurus. Be practical in life."

"Mom, did you give me the authority to stop you when you moved out, leaving me alone with that bastard? I did not control your life. Please stop controlling mine."

Realizing that there was no point arguing with her, George finally relented. *Maybe going away to India would make her better.* "Since you have made up your mind, I will arrange for it. Tell me when you want to leave?" George reconciled.

She was determined to find a guru and the rest was history...

"Are you against sex?" This pointed question coming from Sarah compelled Arun to put down his morning newspaper.

"What kind of sex are you talking about?"

She blushed. In spite of being born in a country, where people discuss sex like food, she could find no word to describe sex!

"I am talking about normal man and woman sex." "You think I am gay?"

She blushed once again.

"Just in case your mind was inquisitive about that possibility, let me clarify that I am not."

"Ever since you have promoted me, I find myself becoming increasingly useless. I don't understand. Then what exactly do you expect of me?" exclaimed Sarah exasperated.

"That's exactly how you felt when you joined as a farm worker too.

Do you remember that?" reminded Arun. "I had a field supervisor to guide me at that time," Sarah argued politely. "Why do you presume that I will not guide you?" Arun looked at her quizzically with a mysterious look in his eyes. Sarah appeared baffled. "Yes, that is true, but I do not understand your guidance either. I wish you could give me a kind of timetable and a 'to do' list."

True desire to please others comes from the heart and not from the head. "I cannot order you. I can only inspire you," Arun continued. "How?" Sarah was getting slightly impatient now. "Think about a good time you had in the recent past."

"The dinner, of course! The yummy pasta you made that night. How can I forget? That was a great surprise." Sarah had a twinkle in her eyes.

"So, how did you feel about the entire experience?" Arun gently asked.

"Tell me Sarah, what pleased you about that dinner?"

With every question, Sarah felt Arun coming closer and closer to her as if he was conveying something of great importance.

"Everything. Your choice, the menu, the planning, the presentation, the music you selected, the fragrance in the room, the lamp... I will not forget that evening. It is the most memorable time I have had in my life." Sarah's hand gestures, body language, expressions on her face, all seemed to flood with excitement as her mind drifted back to those magical moments. "If you ever felt like reciprocating, what would you do?" Arun asked, hoping that Sarah would get the point correctly this time. "Can I repeat the same event?" Sarah replied spontaneously but realized that she had goofed up.

"Sarah! Think creatively." Arun was trying to hide his frustration.

"You don't want me to touch you. You don't like me talking too much. You hardly eat. I rarely see you listening to music. Tell me, how the hell do you expect me to please you? You're impossible!" Sarah made no attempt to hide her frustration.

After a long pregnant pause, Arun asked her, "All right, forget about me.

Do you know what pleases you?"

"Of course! I love bathing in the river, the Gangubai's gentle massage, Mexican food, Jazz music and Wine. No. No wine now.

I have given it up long back," she replied hastily.

"Great! Spend a week pleasing yourself." Arun left the dining room and started climbing the staircase to go to his room.

She started climbing the staircase behind him, thoroughly confused. “What? Do you mean to say you are going to pay me to please myself? What will you gain out of it?”

“A lot. You won’t understand.” He came down a few steps to reach out to her level and put both his palms on her shoulders and looked at her with a lot of love.

“So, you are on your job from today. Tell me, what would you like to do today?” Arun asked sincerely.

“You mean to say, a job of pleasing myself?” She tried swallowing this surprise. A part of her could not believe it. She was just hoping that it did not turn out to be some sort of cruel joke on her. Eventually she gathered some courage to open her mouth once again. “Well, shall I call Gangubai for a massage?”

Gangubai was a herb healer and also the local masseuse. All the new-borns and the new mothers in the village had received their first massage through Gangubai’s skilled hands.

“Sure.”

“I can’t believe this. Are you sure you are not playing some sort of a joke on me?” She stepped down two steps on the staircase with her right index finger in her mouth looking at Arun suspiciously.

“Are you sure you have stopped playing ‘poor me’?” Arun often asked questions rather than answering.

We are so conditioned by our previous experiences, that when life offers a different window of opportunity, we just refuse to see it.

"I got it." She realized that the 'poor me' child in her was out to play another game.

"Thanks." Arun meant what he said, "Go ahead and indulge."

Embracing the unknown with total faith and an open heart is always an ecstatic experience.

Gangubai came in with heated herbal oil in a bowl. Sarah had a wonderful 'champi' followed by a long hot-water bath as Gangubai vigorously scrubbed her back and her feet.

Sarah felt so relaxed after her bath that she drifted off into a gentle slumber even before Gangubai pulled the curtain shut to create a peaceful and serene atmosphere in the room.

When she finished her nap, Arun was waiting for her in the hall. "Let's go," he said, picking up the car key from the key holder on the wall. "Where?" Sarah asked, looking surprised. "Follow me." He liked to keep it short and sweet.

The driver had taken out the jeep rather than his sports car this time. Arun chose to drive himself and she took the seat next to him. It was not that she had never travelled next to him in his car but this time she could not understand the subtle thrill she got. He kept driving leisurely, as if allowing the vehicle to meander around on the roads on its own. Initially they drove through stony, uneven roads right in the middle of the fields. Gradually, the scenery around started changing, the fields started fading out and in a short while the car began zipping effortlessly on the highway.

"Sarah, rather than wasting your time guessing where we are going, why don't you take some time off to enjoy the beauty around you?" He continued driving and Sarah was speechless for a change. "There are so many things on the way you could enjoy watching."

"I realized what I missed when we hit the concrete highway." Sarah said with a tone of regret in her voice.

"There is beauty on the highway too." Arun was in a great mood. "On the highway?" Sarah turned to him with surprise.

"Yes, black colored beauty, white colored beauty, red colored beauty..." he would have gone on but Sarah interrupted.

"You mean to say these cars?" "Why not? Ask those who love cars."

Suddenly the car took a sharp turn and they were in a swanky mall. Arun deftly parked the car and as they alighted, he guided her to a restaurant on the top floor.

"Are we having lunch outside today?" "Yes, Mexican lunch."

She jumped with excitement. *If this is the kind of job he is talking about, sure I love it. I hope he makes this my permanent job profile.*

This is the human mind - rather than enjoying the bliss of the moment, we spend a lot of time worrying about the availability of the same opportunities in the future or regretting not having had them in the past.

Yet, ***interestingly most of us think that we are fairly intelligent to handle our lives well!***

Obviously, the child in Sarah had surfaced at the thought of Mexican food.

They spent the rest of the day shopping at the mall. She was amazed at how he could patiently guide her through her shopping. After a long time, she found herself getting interested in perfumes and accessories. Initially she felt guilty splurging and indulging, but Arun remained firmly insistent.

On their way back they stopped at the seaside. Sarah found herself sitting contentedly on the beach, sipping coconut water and watching the sunset. Arun was gazing into the horizon.

"I can't believe this. I couldn't have been happier." Suddenly a streak of sadness came and went. Arun noticed it.

"Did you think of something from the past?" Arun tried inquiring in a gentle manner.

"Yes. My vacation with Dad in the Bahamas... That is where he slept with me for the first time." Sarah wanted to tell him everything.

"You mean you actually had a physical relationship with him?" Arun felt puzzled but quickly curtailed his judgmental response, fearing that it might inhibit her from venting her repressed emotions.

A judgmental response and unwarranted advice are the biggest foes of good communication.

"Yes," she said with a long sigh. "A one-off occasion?"

"No. It went on for a long time, a few years," she looked down as she narrated some of the incidents.

"Is this the pain that you are trying to escape from?" Arun inquired, wrinkling his forehead.

"Perhaps. Let's get up." She wanted to cut it short now.

"Tell me how many men besides your dad have you slept with?" Arun wanted to know everything.

"I have lost count." Sarah said with a resigned tone. "I would sleep with anybody who indulged me.

I have slept for money, a good dinner, a good dress, perfume... party... vacation... anything that my mind craved for at that moment."

"Sarah, is it necessary to be so critical about your past? We all are taught to barter in life. They say there are no free lunches. Not just lunches... perhaps nothing is free!" Arun tried comforting her with his words.

Nothing is free because we firmly believe so.

By chance, if someone offers us something without expecting anything in return, we start suspecting the motive.

"I went into the 'You please me, I please you' mode with so many men one after the other."

"Then?"

"I got fed up... I got fed up with sleeping with the men...I got fed up with the things men could buy for women. My heart started searching for something different but I didn't know what. All I know is that there is a deep void in my heart."

Arun remained silent.

It is very easy to help others emotionally offload; all you need is to be a patient and neutral listener.

"My search for a guru is the result of all these things. I wish someone could tell me what it is that I am searching for." She paused for a while as her life seemed to flow away along with her tears.

"I am tired, Arun. I am really tired of life."

Arun put his arms around her with a lot of affection as they returned to the car.

They had dinner at a roadside 'Dhaba,' sitting on a rustic cot.

Both of them spent this time quietly, hardly exchanging more than a few words, although it felt as if they had communicated a lot.

The loudness of communication is directly proportional to the emotional distance between individuals. When two individuals feel close to each other they hardly need to whisper and when they feel terribly distanced, they resort to screaming and shouting and yet fail to make themselves understood.

What is it? Why this strange feeling? Sarah asked herself without bothering to get an answer.

"Arun, thanks," returning back home, she broke the silence.

She gently put her right palm on his shoulder and whispered softly, "By saying what I said to you, I have taken a huge load off my chest. I am feeling much lighter." She continued thanking him with a sincere expression of gratitude in her eyes. "Thanks." She said it once more with an isolated teardrop rolling down from her right eye.

"You are welcome, dear."

He gave her a very warm hug outside her room and kissed her forehead.

“Good night, Sarah.” “Good night, Arun.”

The next morning Sarah awoke very early, feeling very fresh.

She wore a flowing peacock blue dress with a floral design and a wonderful embroidered neckline along with matching bangles and earrings.

She watered the indoor plants, plucked flowers from the farm and arranged them neatly in a mud vase.

Then she looked out for scented incense and lit one in the central part of the house.

She went to the dining room and selected a track of light Indian classical music and went to the kitchen to make a cup of mint tea for Arun.

The tea smelt really good with freshly plucked mint leaves. She had chosen beautiful earthen cups to serve tea garnished with mint leaves. She asked the butler about Arun’s preference for breakfast and instructed him to make some ‘Aloo Parathas’ with mango ‘lassi’.

She went with two cups of mint tea to Arun’s room. She entered without any hesitation today. He had just woken up.

Smelling the fragrance of the mint tea, he sprang up in the bed to grab his cup. She joined him too. “Would you like some cookies with tea, Arun?”

“No. Not with the morning cup of tea.” Arun was busy sipping the tea.

Arun was giving the tea his full attention. "Ramu Chacha was right." She smiled. "Oh! So, you inquired about all that?" "Why not? Isn't it part of my job profile?" She was surprised with her own confidence. "Of course, yes."

"Do you like mint tea, Sarah?"

"No. Back in America, I used to guzzle black coffee every hour to keep awake."

"Now?" "Now I have stopped it, especially after coming to the farmhouse." "Umm"

"I don't need so much caffeine because I have many more reasons and ways to keep awake."

Both of them smiled. They remained silent, enjoying the remaining tea. "Can I visit your bathroom?" Sarah interrupted the silence.

"Oh, sure."

She went inside. She arranged the bath linen neatly, took out a fresh bar of soap and arranged it next to the tub. She left the tap on to fill up the bathtub with warm water.

"I will be back in a moment," she declared as she went down carrying the empty teacups. Arun kept watching her movements with a delightedly astonished look. She quickly returned with colorful flowers in a basket. She arranged some in an earthen pot lying on an old carved wooden table. She sat on the sofa and separated the petals of the roses. Arun kept watching with great interest, this engrossed beauty so involved in his room.

"I have prepared the bath in case you feel like soaking yourself right now." The bathtub really looked inviting as the rose petals interspersed with the foam in the bathtub.

Sarah was surprised to see him come out of the bathroom in such a hurry.

She wondered if he had even dipped his body in the tub.

Arun of course did not want to let her know that watching her in his room was much more interesting than the petal filled bathtub.

Sarah had already selected his clothes for the day. "Today, when you go for a visit to the farm, I will organize your wardrobe if you are fine with it." She declared with confidence.

"Of course, dear. I've been waiting for someone to do this for me for a long time." He had come out of the bathroom with just a towel wrapped around his hips. Sarah felt a deep arousal on seeing his semi-naked body but pretended to remain unruffled as if the woman in her was unaffected by his bare chest.

He waited with his palms resting above his hip joints.

Arun did not have to say anything but Sarah understood his body language, which suggested that he expected her to leave the room so that he could change comfortably. She smiled with joy and left the room.

When he came down for breakfast, he was more than delighted to find the table laden with flowers and the fragrance of sandalwood incense in the air. The sweet melody of santoor added to the morning bliss. Looks like the magic is working, Arun chuckled, as he settled down to have his breakfast.

How did she know Aloo Parathas are my favorite breakfast? Arun made no attempt to hide his delight.

Sarah was very happy with herself and her newfound creativity. All she wanted in return was a softer approach from Arun. An all-acknowledging smile and occasional warm hug...that was enough to keep her going.

By the end of the week, the entire farmhouse had a new look. She changed the colours of the walls, the curtains, the upholstery... almost everything. She even bought a hand painted crockery set and antique pieces.

"Sarah, can you please keep the bathtub ready so that I can soak myself? I am feeling really tired tonight," Arun called as his car approached the farmhouse.

With the help of Gangubai, she had found some effective and relaxing herbal preparations for an oil massage. She kept them ready for him in case he agreed for a body or foot massage.

From her frequent massages from Gangubai, Sarah had picked up a few strokes and techniques, which she was more than willing to experiment on Arun's body.

"What about dinner, Arun?"

"No, I am not hungry. I had dinner at the business meeting. You finish yours before I come so that we can spend some time chatting," Arun continued talking to her on the phone while driving on the highway.

"Would you join me for dessert at least?" Sarah pleaded.

"Ok, what's for dessert?" Arun conceded.

"I have made caramel custard. I've tried, but I don't know how it has turned out," she sounded modest. Nevertheless, Arun heard the excitement in her voice.

"Sure. Let me come home and then I will give you my feedback."

He came when she was about to finish her meal. She got up and greeted him with a warm hug. For a change Sarah was not worried about his curt behavior.

"Would you like to have the custard now?" asked Sarah with enthusiasm. "Sure." Arun settled down on the chair near the dining table.

"Sarah, I am feeling quite full," Arun politely explained as he rubbed his right palm on his slightly bloated stomach. "Can we share some of yours?" asked Arun. Sarah could smell the rum on his breath. Hmm...He even looked a bit tipsy. She wondered how many pegs he had needed to get drunk. She fantasized about him completely drunk and kissing her all over. Unwillingly she shook herself out of her fantasies, out of the fear of her mind being read by Arun once again.

"My pleasure," she said with a sensuous look on her face. He looked at her to find out whether her response came merely as a courtesy or if she had really meant what she had said. He said nothing but kept looking at her eyes.

"I mean it," Sarah confirmed with emphasis as she started feeling a bit uncomfortable.

"I know," he simply nodded. She did not reply and watched him eat the dessert from her plate.

As Arun entered his room, he noticed a wooden bowl containing oil placed on the side table, a thick bath towel and a few small towels neatly arranged on the bed.

"What is this, Sarah?" "You said you were tired so I thought a massage would be a great idea. You could still choose otherwise," she shrugged her shoulders gently, throwing the ball in his court.

"Wow! I was thinking about it. Tell me where you want me to lie down?" He started unbuttoning his shirt. To see him inhibition-free was a welcome change. *Probably because of the booze*, she thought.

"Where would you be comfortable?" Sarah chose to question in reply to his question.

"I will be comfortable in your lap," said Arun while removing his belt. She tried hiding her thrill, but the change in the color of her cheeks betrayed her.

"It is part of my job, Arun. Whatever you say."

For the first time Arun sincerely wished she had not mentioned the word 'job.'

When a preprogrammed machine does not necessarily perform as per expectation at all points of time...

Why expect humans to do so?

Sarah settled down on the bed with her legs crossed and Arun put his head on her lap. His crown was settled in close proximity to her pelvis and there was a crazy movement there.

She kept reminding herself that this is a part of her job and continued, lightly massaging his head. "Sarah, could you get me to sleep like this, daily? You have marvelous hands," Arun muttered half asleep.

I have marvelous legs too, she thought but did not say it aloud. Arun raised his head slightly and glanced at her legs.

Oops! How embarrassing! She bit her lip. *This means even if I feel aroused, he is able to catch that. God, this is dangerous, and I don't want it anymore. But how long will I keep escaping my feelings?*

"Arun, it feels good to have a man's touch on my body."

"It feels great to have a beautiful woman take care of me like this. Thank you so much for everything. Even if you leave tomorrow, I will have great memories to cherish."

She put her fingers on his lips. "Please don't talk about parting. I am looking forward to a long-term relationship."

"So, you are sure that you will get an extension and promotion in your job?"

She laughed but seriously wished he did not keep reminding her that she was simply satisfying her job requirements.

From then on, it became a daily routine for Arun to have a massage at bedtime. They kept changing positions in bed to increase their physical proximity. She spent the better part of her evenings standing in front of the mirror critically assessing her sensuous appeal.

One night as Sarah prepared to give him a massage, he gently placed his hand over hers as if he was about to say something important. His eyes were filled with gratitude as he spoke, "Sarah, you have no idea, how wonderful it is to have this tender touch just before sleeping. Thank you for everything." He smiled as he closed his eyes.

Sarah said nothing even though Arun's expression of gratitude dampened her spirit. Why can't he choose a different way to express his gratitude? She sighed and as usual he picked up her thoughts. "How about me giving you a massage tonight, Sarah?"

For a few seconds, she held her breath as pleasurable vibes ran through her body. But then immediately she feared his withdrawal from the proposal. So, she quickly glanced at his face to examine his response. She saw that he was serious indeed.

"Tell me how you want me to go about it?" Sarah asked, sitting on his bed.

"I will start with your feet. You can lie down." *I wish he starts with my breasts*, she thought. For a change she wished that he would read her mind. And he did.

"Are you not comfortable about the feet?" asked Arun trying to hide the mischief in his eyes.

"My entire body is craving for your touch, so go ahead."

The next few moments were magical. How intuitively he knew his strokes! There was something soothing about his touch. She waited in anticipation for him to reach her breasts. She expected fireworks but nothing happened. She wondered how Arun's touch was not arousing her as much as she had anticipated....

Touch conveys more than words.

For Arun the need for touch was beyond physical intimacy, but this starved tigress yearned for something different.

The westerner in her could not fathom the very idea of not getting aroused in spite of terrific desire.

Strange. He has definitely got to be gay. She thought.

As usual Arun read her thoughts and Sarah knew about it. His fingers strongly objected to her judgment and now wanted to prove the contrary. The 'yang' counterpart in him did not find any reason to remain suppressed and what followed was an ethereal experience for both.

No one in the past had aroused her the way he did.

She paused suddenly considering the possibility of this entire experience being an illusion.

Many of us believe that good things in life happen only in dreams. No wonder people become alive when they are dreaming and sleep when life is offering a great opportunity.

Arun whispered in her ears, "You know, Sarah, it's been so painful to let you leave this bed every night, after being physically so close."

On hearing this, Sarah jumped on him with joy and kissed him on his lips.

Finally, she had received a verbal confirmation that Arun was interested in her as a woman.

"Sarah," Arun moved her closer to him as she was leaving the bed to collect her scattered clothes on the floor, "Will you share my bedroom?"

She nodded. "This is not a part of your job profile. This is a personal request. You really don't have to continue with the job. Please don't look at this offer as a kind of barter." He was trying to make himself clear as he held her very close in his arms.

She said nothing for the next few minutes and kept moving her fingers sensuously all over his chest.

"You have not responded to what I said," Arun impatiently interrupted. "I did, with my touch. Doesn't that say it all?" Sarah had a style of conveying her feelings which Arun was beginning to love. He chose not to reply and continued enjoying her fingers moving on his hairy chest.

For the next few days, they behaved like a dating couple, exploring each other's body and mind, trying to touch each other at the soul level. No stones were left unturned to make each other happy.

One evening as they watched the sunset, relaxing on the garden swing, Arun asked "Sarah, are you happy?"

She nodded her head. "Very much. I feel content and very much at peace with myself."

"Tell me something more about your life here. How do you feel being in this farmhouse?"

"Great! I couldn't have asked for anything better," Sarah said with enthusiasm in her voice.

"Given a choice now, Sarah, would you go back on your search for a guru?"

"I am still searching for my guru, Arun, but not in the outside world, I am searching for one within. I am experiencing a constant voice inside me who is guiding me on what to do and what not to do."

"Yes! When did you get in touch with this voice, Sarah?" "The first time that we made love." She blushed.

"I was so confused. I did not know if I was doing the right thing.

A voice said 'Go ahead Sarah, it is all right. He is your right partner'. It was a surreal experience, that of being connected to you, to me, to the entire universe," she continued.

"Arun, what more could I have asked for? Something which I felt was so earthly, gave me such a spiritual experience."

Though she was talking aloud, essentially, Sarah was still in her contemplative mood. "Why then do so many gurus abstain from sex? Not only do they abstain but they also promote abstinence actively and emphatically."

"I only know about their promotion of abstinence, but I have no clue if they really abstain or not!" he smiled mischievously.

Sarah stared at him with eyes wide open. In her wild search for a guru, she had come across some who had made sexual advances at her. But she had chosen to ignore all those thoughts.

"Arun, I am serious. I don't understand all this. Please explain it to me." "Why don't you ask the voices inside you?" Arun genuinely meant that. "All right, I did ask and the answer was that ***the act of union could be divine. It depends upon who you unite with and the intent behind the union***," she said in a very serious tone.

"If you sleep," Arun took up from where she left, "with an intention of temporary gratification, you will get exactly that. If you sleep with some personal gain in mind you will get that exactly. If you sleep to please your partner, you will achieve that. If you sleep to overpower your partner, you will experience that too. You can sleep with someone to express yourself, to express love, to achieve some higher goal in mind or simply to feel one with your partner in that moment."

It is a great experience to feel one and connected with the entire world. However, one may start by feeling one with a partner and later transcend the relationship and extrapolate this experience to feel the same way with the entire world.

"I chose the last. The experience of a sense of oneness with you led me to experience oneness with the universe."

"Is this what Osho preached? I always kept away from his literature. Perhaps I was not ready for it," said Sarah. "I had suppressed my desire because of my past experiences of saturation, and partly because of my so-called spiritual beliefs, but Arun, that is my story, tell me about you," she paused and then continued.

"Tell me, Arun, about the women in your life, besides me that is," she joked.

He stiffened his body slightly. "Okay, then tell me who was that lucky one?" "Her name is Dipti. She is a very special woman in my life."

Sarah felt a sharp pain in her chest. *Don't tell me that like my father he too has used me to fill the gap. All these days when he used to keep disappearing, was he going to be with her? I don't want to know more about it.* This riot of thoughts swept through her mind.

"She is coming tomorrow. I am going to receive her at the airport. Would you like to join me?"

"Oh no! Thanks."

That night, Sarah's entire body was hurting. Her head was splitting and she spent the night in utter restlessness.

The next day, Arun got up very early to go to the airport. "Tell me, which shirt would you like to see me in?" "The light purple one."

"Thanks, Sarah, will you take it out for me? Will it go well with the beige trousers?"

"No, the off-white ones will be more suitable." "All right, I will wear exactly that." He started wearing the shirt. "Choose a good perfume, Sarah." He was busy dressing up without noticing her inner turmoil.

"Tell me if my gelled hair is looking good?" Sarah's body stiffened with every question, but she complied.

"If he can read every thought of mine, why can't he read my agony?" she thought in her mind.

"It would be a good idea if you come along too, Sarah. Dipti would be very happy to see you," he said while leaving the room.

"Does she know about me?" she asked. "No, I wanted to give her a surprise."

Ramu Chacha entered the room with two cups of tea and breakfast. They sipped their tea quietly, lost in their own thoughts.

"Are you ready for the next step now?"

Her heart missed a beat in that one second. She optimistically thought, *he is going to talk about marriage!*

"Sarah, get ready to discuss your next promotion."

The next promotion? What? And I thought you were seriously involved with me. You are still seeing me as an employee.

She felt like screaming on top of her voice. But she restrained herself from saying anything. She reminded herself - *no escaping and no self-sabotage. I need to survive. I need to thrive.*

"I am."

"This is a special job offer that I would not offer to any Tom, Dick or Harry."

She changed the tone of her voice and said, "Tell me about my next promotion."

"Let me come back from the airport."

"Thank you for the promotion."

I guess I will catch up on my sleep in the meanwhile. She went back to bed as Arun left the room.

When the reality of life gets too painful to face, we often resort to the dream world to salvage and recoup. Sarah unknowingly did the same.

Chapter Three

Sarah prepared the breakfast table for three and waited for them to arrive.

She saw Arun getting out of the car to escort a charming young woman on his arm. She seemed to be very happy to have arrived here.

Sarah admired her sense of dressing and choice of accessories as she scanned her from head to toe.

In spite of intense resistance, Sarah somehow managed to welcome the newcomer with poise.

The abundant joy and bliss of the last few days seemed to have vanished overnight. Can an unknown presence make so much of a difference in my life? Sarah wondered at how volatile feelings can be.

True joy and happiness are trapped beneath our layers of conditioning. The human race is unable to fathom the idea of being happy for the sake of being happy. It has conditioned itself to be temporarily happy only under desired circumstances.

For example, when there is money, comfort, success, love, recognition, etc. The irony is that all that we have yearned for eventually begins to lose its value and we start a fresh new cycle in search of other parameters, which we assume will lead us to happiness. If we can momentarily stop chasing the means to happiness and take a pause to believe that the experience of joy will be enough, we can get rid of a whole lot of unnecessary grind.

Happy are those who choose happiness as a constant companion rather than chase the means to get it.

Dipti came in and took a good look at Sarah. "Dipti, meet Sarah, our new farmhouse manager. Sarah, meet Dipti, a very special woman in my life, the co-owner of this estate and...my elder sister."

There was visible relief on Sarah's face. The energy levels shot up as she stepped forward to greet her.

Suddenly, it was okay that he had not acknowledged her as the woman in his life. Now there appeared to be some hope, some possibility, perhaps.

How much the human mind wants to live in a hopeful state of mind!

Hope is that lubricant which helps us glide smoothly towards the future, especially when we are on a sticky wicket.

Dipti went up to her room which was adjacent to Arun's. Sarah had always seen this room locked. Everyone in the house had strict instructions not to enter the room without Arun's permission. Although she never inquired about it, she always wondered what was so special about the room. Sarah was already beginning to dislike Dipti's presence and proximity to Arun, but she had no choice in the matter.

Arun followed Dipti to her room and closed the door behind him. Sarah overheard them arguing, but she managed to quietly wait for them to come out.

Her eyes were still fixed on the closed door. She hated herself for feeling insecure but she could not help wanting Arun's undivided attention. Arun seemed to dote on Dipti, and Sarah now feared that if his sister did not approve of her, she would have to leave the farmhouse.

Our fearful thoughts actually energize the possibility of a dreaded event. That is how we invariably invite situations that we fear the most.

Sarah eventually invited what she feared the most. In two days, Dipti began becoming more and more critical of Sarah. She did not approve of the many changes this 'other' woman had made in her house. She found out from the servants that Sarah had been sharing her dear brother's bedroom.

Dipti kept Arun occupied and involved in conversations with her most of the time. Both of them would go out for morning walks and chat late into the night.

Sarah started feeling neglected. She felt totally cut off from Arun. She had to wait for hours to grab some time with him without Dipti.

Arun started noticing the stress brought on by the feminine intimidation which both of them felt due to each other's presence in the house.

Sarah started dreading the possibility of being uprooted once again. Her stomach would churn every time she saw Dipti.

Dipti's insecurity was gradually showing up in rude behavior. When something happened in front of Arun, he had to keep quiet to maintain diplomacy.

I can't take it anymore, but I don't feel like going away from Arun either.

Sarah felt torn.

One day she was sitting all alone in the guest room, when Arun walked in after a late-night chat with Dipti.

"You shouldn't have moved out of my room."

"I am sure your sister doesn't like me sharing your room." Sarah looked down and continued, "I bet she is upset about it."

"She will take time, Sarah, because she is very possessive about me. After our parents died, we had only each other for support, so the bonding is very deep."

"I don't think so. If that was really the case, she would not be so insecure about my presence in the house," Sarah was soft but firm in her opinion.

Arun kept quiet. He simply put his head in her lap and fell asleep on her bed. It filled her with warmth, as she missed cuddling him in her sleep.

Sarah had said something very important. The insecurity about a relationship is inversely proportional to the faith in your bonding with your partner. ***The insecurities in life reflect the need for faith in one's own self.***

In the morning when he tried making love to her, her body stiffened a bit. He perceived this as her resistance, left her alone in the bed and joined Dipti for a morning walk.

"Arun, from where have you picked up this girl? She looks like a whore to me. You know men are very vulnerable to women during and after sex. You should keep away from this woman until you are sure about her intentions and character." Dipti was determined to protect Arun from Sarah.

"She is here to find some spiritual answers, Dipti."

"What kind of spiritual answers? What is she doing here? Don't tell me you are planning to become her guru."

"Me, and guru! What nonsense! Dipti, forget about her. Let's talk about you and the guys in your life. Tell me, what happened to Sam, whom I met when I came to LA the last time?" Arun tried distracting her to avoid further argument.

"Arun don't digress from the topic. I am serious. Pack this girl off from this house right now! I am serious... I don't find her genuine. Something is fishy somewhere. The servants told me that she was sharing the bedroom with you before I arrived? Why did she have to put on a show and shift out? What is she trying to prove?"

"Dipti, get off her back. Let's enjoy the walk."

Dipti's hostility increased. She started treating Sarah as excess baggage.

Arun could not convince her otherwise and the rift widened.

Why the hell is Arun overruling my wishes for this 'firang'? He doesn't claim to love her, nor does he have any intention to settle in with her. He appears to have no affection for her, then why? Dipti could not understand.

Sarah too found herself struggling with Dipti's authority in the house. She secretly started wishing that Dipti would leave at the earliest. She felt stuck. She could not understand why Arun's dynamics with her should change because of Dipti's presence. She was disappointed that he had even stopped coming to her room.

Arun could not understand the rivalry. There was no overlapping in their positions. Why should he go through repeated rejection from Sarah? *She leaves the room as and when she fancies, she remains emotionally and physically unavailable, what the hell is happening to this bloody woman?* There was a lot of silent anger, but no time to talk. Dipti would ensure that Sarah did not get any free time with Arun.

The vulnerable man in Arun dreaded the possibility of further rejection from his sweetheart and her stiffening up on his approach.

It's crazy, Sarah was probably right. Dipti is not really as secure about me as I would like to believe. Or else her love would have allowed me the freedom to live my life as per my will.

Dipti cancelled her holiday with her friends in the Maldives because she feared that she had to set Sarah straight. She tried her best to make sensitive Sarah feel rejected and humiliated so that she felt physically and emotionally uncomfortable in the house.

"Dipti, don't do this to her. She has nobody to fall back on," Arun appealed.

"You mean to say that you have opened up a home for the destitute?" "Dipti, try to understand, I love her." "What? I can't believe this. You're confused, you don't know what you are talking about.

She doesn't even look at you, she is in her own world! Arun, she's a selfish bitch and you must get rid of her."

Dipti was almost screaming, her upper body leaning towards him. He had not seen Dipti use such an aggressive posture and tone.

"She is trying to win you over with her sob story. Have you told her that you love her?"

"No. I haven't."

"What kind of relationship is that? Does she love you?"

"Yes, but I don't know if she loves me the way I want her to love me." Arun tried his best to be patient with her.

Suddenly there was a knock on the door. Sarah entered visibly disturbed.

With wary politeness she declared that she needed to talk to Arun alone. "What is it?" asked Arun.

"It is about my job," replied Sarah as she firmly stood near the door.

"If it is about the job, you can talk about it in front of me. I am the co-owner of this estate." Dipti's hand gesture conveyed a lot of arrogance.

"Sorry Ma'am, it is he who appointed me; therefore, I will be submitting my resignation and parting words to him. But before I do that, I want to speak to him alone for a while."

"Sorry you will not. You can leave your resignation letter and leave."

She left the letter on the table. After calmly closing the door behind her, she ran to her room to avoid showing her tears. She was extremely hurt. She had decided not to play her 'poor me' card with anyone. And she was going to stick by it!

The situation is becoming unbearable. I can't keep taking this all the time. She treats me worse than she treats the servants. She argued with herself in order to justify her resignation.

She kept her mind singularly on justifying her resignation. ***The mind has a crazy need to justify all the actions we have taken in the past, all the actions we are taking in the now and every decision we have taken for the future. But there is a difference between justification and the truth. Very few of us have the courage to face the truth. The truth is independent of justification.***

If Arun showed Sarah the slightest attention, Dipti would get more revengeful than before. Sarah now dreaded even looking at Arun, living in the perpetual fear of showdowns all the time. She did not know what comment would be thrown at her and under what circumstances.

Arun went to Sarah's room, overruling Dipti's strong protest. She was sobbing aloud. Arun put his hand on her back and said, "Don't cry Sarah, I know you can handle this."

"I'm sorry," she spoke softly, wiping her tears. "I had no intention to show my tears or to play 'poor me' again." Sarah was visibly struggling to keep her dignity in those painful moments.

“You are not playing this card of ‘self-pity’ with me but with your own self.

What is it? Why are you wallowing in self-pity?” asked Arun.

“I am not,” she tried defending herself.

“Of course, you are. Otherwise, Dipti wouldn’t treat you the way she is treating you.”

Arun was right. ***Others treat us the way we treat ourselves. If you need others to change their behavior towards you, change your own behavior towards yourself.***

But of course, we do not want to understand this fact.

It is very easy to blame others for what is happening to us. And we always go for the seemingly easier choices in life and make life more difficult in the bargain.

“She is your sister, so you are taking up for her.” She pulled a long face. “All right, she is my sister. But who is she to you?” Arun asked calmly. “No one.”

“Then why are you letting her affect you?” Arun reasoned with her. She kept quiet.

“Why are you quitting?” He wanted Sarah to look at the situation threadbare.

“Because I want to be relieved and be free once more.”

“Sarah, ***if anything traps you, it is your ignorance and the emotions arising out of that ignorance. And if you are genuinely seeking freedom, seek emotional freedom by being aware of your restricting and emotionally disturbing thoughts.***”

Arun lashed out a few more facts, "The moment you respond to her games, she stands the possibility of winning the game and you risk losing your game."

The only way others can win against you is when you choose to play with them, be it the game of relationships. If no one plays, no one wins. But it is so hard not to play, because we have an inherent need to take up challenges in life.

He left the room abruptly to give Sarah the time to swallow these pearls of wisdom.

Dipti kept waiting for her to leave but Sarah was very much there, showing up finally at dinner time.

"Haven't you left yet?" Dipti continued in her offensive tone.

"I find no need to leave now." Sarah gently shrugged her shoulders and maintained her polite behavior, but Dipti was in no mood to listen to this.

Arun interrupted Dipti, "I am thinking of promoting her to the position of estate manager. Our current manager has gone on leave for two months. I think Sarah will fit the profile very well. The way she has managed the house, I have no doubt that she will be able to handle the estate too." Arun tried appearing optimistic, but patiently waited for her response.

"There is a lot of difference between managing a house and an estate. But if you think she can manage, let's try it out."

Dipti was visibly relieved because the estate manager had separate accommodation. She presumed that Sarah would shift there.

But when Sarah did not shift, Dipti was terribly disappointed. Arun's response was, "The previous manager has not yet vacated the place. If his issues at home are settled, he might think of coming back."

Dipti felt more frustrated than ever. The duo started leaving the house in the morning together, for the farms. Their work kept them together for the better part of the day. Sarah's new promotion had added dignity to her demeanor.

Dipti kept canceling all her appointments and programs hoping to 'set things right' between Sarah and Arun.

The emotional independence experiment worked very well for Sarah, though at times she found it difficult to maintain neutrality in Dipti's presence.

"I still shudder when I look at her," she shared her thoughts with honesty. Arun and Sarah would often snatch some beautiful moments while driving on the rough stony pathways of the farmhouse.

"Who is making her an authority figure? Who is giving her authority?" "Me? Tell me Arun, why do I go through this emotional mess?"

It is very difficult to accept that we are responsible for the mess in our lives.

"Tell me one great woman figure who has not suffered?" Arun questioned.

So many women entertain the belief that they have to suffer in order to become a heroine in their own eyes.

At least in Indian mythology, most women have gone through suffering. Some of them are regularly worshipped by the present generation. They are the role models for many women."

Sarah gave him a look of disbelief.

"Why do you think soap operas do so well everywhere? All they show is suffering and struggle at various levels. Most women identify with the characters! Suffering has become a part of a woman's psyche. They suffer in the name of love. They suffer while raising their children. They suffer in the name of sacrifice. They suffer at the hands of their fathers, their sons and their male counterparts. The more they suffer, the more they glorify their suffering." Arun was breathless with his agitated outburst. Sarah had never seen him so upset.

"What could they have done?" asked Sarah.

"***Women could have chosen not to suffer.***" Arun was very sure of what he was saying.

"How can one choose not to suffer? Isn't it natural? Isn't suffering induced by the pains from one's surroundings?" Sarah had her own doubts.

"***The pain may be inevitable, but suffering is a choice one exercises.***" Arun was glad that she had asked this question. He moved into the driver's seat explaining to her with a lot of love and compassion.

"Life gives us a lot of opportunities to choose from, you could choose either to suffer or to accept the challenges of life with joy." Arun continued.

"But others are out to hurt, like your sister." A part of her did not want to agree with him.

"Even if she is out to hurt," Arun interrupted impatiently before Sarah could go into her 'poor me' state, "Why did you let that happen to you? The day you stopped; the events took a turn for the better. Out of the blue, I got the idea of promoting and shifting you out of her zone for a while," he said emphatically.

"Do you still want to move away from her?" asked Arun to reconfirm. "No," replied Sarah, "I have decided not to run away from anything in life."

"Oh! So that's the reason why you don't want to leave?" Arun concluded. "No. The reason I don't want to leave is..." she choked and looked away. "...Is?" Arun prompted leaning closer to her.

He geared himself to finally listen to the words he had so craved for. "Because...."

"Because?"

"Because I love you and can't bear to be away from you anymore," Sarah said in one breath and waited for him to respond.

He quietly put his left arm around her, while effortlessly continuing to drive the car at a high speed.

When you utter the words 'I love you' to someone for the first time, it brings in tremendous joy and relief, but when there is no reciprocation as per our expectations, it leaves us feeling vulnerable to the inevitable - of being ridiculed, rejected, manipulated and many more such fears.

It requires courage to truly love someone, and greater courage to pursue your love with dignity.

Legends of many years are the proof of great pains associated with so-called true love...... No touching love story ended with a 'happily ever after'...... But I don't know whether in this lifetime he will ever disclose his feelings to me.

Thoughts raced through Sarah's mind while Arun was busy racing the car back home.

Sometimes we wonder what love is.

A teenager's infatuation, a mother's sacrifice, a father's sense of responsibility, or indulgently spoiling a child - the meaning of love differs for different people under different circumstances and a different set of past experiences.

We have so many tags, conditions, expectations and presuppositions about love, that true love almost always gets lost in this web of our own making.

It is a beautiful feeling to love someone for the sake of loving and still more wonderful to be loved by someone totally unconditionally, without any tags and expectations attached.

Sarah was on her way to experiencing simultaneously both the depth and the height of her love. But Arun, as always, remained unpredictable.

Chapter Four

Sarah and Arun began to get comfortable in each other's lives once again. Sarah shifted back to Arun's room. She took on the farm manager's role eagerly absorbing all that she could to understand the systems, so that she could deliver her duties impeccably. A common bedroom and a busy work schedule on the farms gave their relationship fertile ground to grow and mature.

Dipti's disappointment and uneasiness increased as she felt extremely alienated. She was unable to reconcile to the fact that her brother, a grown-up man, was entitled to have a woman of his choice in his life.

The human mind always has a need to keep proving certain strong beliefs. The stronger the belief, the more are the chances of its manifestation and every manifestation strengthens that belief. And the cycle repeats.

No wonder so many of us find our lives going round and round in a circle. People change, circumstances change, but the experience remains the same. Very few of us look back to discover the deep connection between the belief and the experience.

Dipti chose to believe that Sarah was responsible for creating a rift between Arun and her.

This she tried proving in various ways to Arun through her repeated nagging and sulking, which proved counterproductive. In order to avoid the unpleasantness which precipitated after each interaction, Arun started capping his conversation.

All games, including the game of life, are the sum total of the moves planned and played out, by its players. If one of the players refuses to play, the other is left with no choice, but to give up or carry on the game with someone else.

When Dipti could not succeed in her attempt to gain control of the situation, out of desperation she openly challenged her brother. "I can't stand this woman!" She appeared annoyed trying to maneuver the situation to suit her needs, making no bones about her dislike for Sarah.

"I have already told you about my feelings towards her," Arun tried to be very calm. He disliked disharmony.

"But something is fishy. You must get rid of her," Dipti continued with her game.

"I think you should get rid of your fixed ideas," Arun started losing his cool.

"Don't you see we never had any differences before this? This woman comes into our lives and manages to create problems for both of us and still you refuse to do anything about it!" Dipti made no attempt to hide her disgust and dislike for Sarah and raised her voice to project her anger. Sitting in Arun's room, Sarah overheard the muffled sounds of Dipti's shrieking, as the agitated sister relentlessly stormed at her brother with offensive arguments.

"Dipti, who's creating the problem between us?" Arun tried his best to hide his agitation, but from the manner in which he was pacing the room, it became very apparent that he was not getting through.

Hurt by her brother's unwillingness to see her point, Dipti desperately blurted out, "Arun I want you to decide between her and me."

We often turn our lives into casinos, where we gamble with our relationships, careers, and prestige. Immature gamblers are immature players of life. They succumb to the fear of failure which makes them gamble to the point of losing the very thing they are attempting to gain.

"Don't be silly, Dipti, you are messing up everything for me. Why can't we love each other and give each other the space to be? After all, where is the overlap? Where is the question of choosing between you and her? Have you gone insane? You are beyond my comprehension."

Life could be perfect and so could the relationship triangles. But perfection could bring in stagnation. So, one of the angles in the triangle plays a fulcrum and desires the conjunction of the other two angles. And of course, the remaining two angles also have the desire to abrade, strike or displace the other, like knobs of two yo-yoing pendulums sharing a single fulcrum point.

It was Arun's desire for a cordial relationship between Sarah and Dipti, coupled with Dipti's desire to displace Sarah; and

Sarah's resilient responses, which were adding interesting angles to the triangle.

"Why am I being questioned about my love for you? This really hurts, Arun. Why can't you understand my feelings?"

"You know we are not going to live like this with each other forever. One fine day we are going to find our own life partners and if we want to remain in a relationship, we will have to understand and accept each other's partners." Arun almost collapsed in the chair.

Sarah felt anxious as she continued listening to the loud arguments between Arun and Dipti on the balcony of the mezzanine floor. She thought of interrupting.

She contemplated leaving the farmhouse in order to prevent further discord between the siblings.

But before her contemplation could come to some meaningful decision, Arun entered the room in a huff and strode towards her. He was breathing hard, with bloodshot eyes and a few beads of sweat on his forehead. He portrayed a very different avatar.

Her guts twitched with unknown anxiety.

"Sarah!" He was panting due to his effort to contain his emotions. "You need to pack your clothes. We are shifting out of this estate."

"What?"

"Yes. Dipti is uncomfortable with your presence." Sarah suddenly felt her energies sink. Her face turned pale and she just collapsed on the bed. It was true that she did not like

Dipti, but the last thing she wanted was to see Arun out of his own farmhouse because of her.

“Arun, it is me who should be going. You don’t really have to shift out of this farmhouse. You love this farm so much! You have worked so hard to nurture it. You have sacrificed your career to look after it. You shouldn’t leave this way.”

“No. These farms are a part of my family inheritance. I have looked after them as any custodian would. It is all right if Dipti wants us to leave. Instead of me, she will now look after them.”

Unable to reply, Sarah remained glued to the edge of the bed. He gently leaned over her. Putting both his palms on her shoulders, he stood close to her. She felt his warm breath on her face. Her eyes refused to blink, time had momentarily frozen. Her dilated pupils vacillated in search of subtle unspoken communication from the abyss of his eyes. Finally, as if in slow motion his lips separated. Arun was about to ask the question that he had been resisting for a long time.

“Sarah, will you marry me?” His heart was beating very fast with the seemingly volatile nature of the moment.

“What?” magically the color returned to her face. She was not prepared for this question. The staring eyes sparkled at the unexpected turn of destiny. Otherwise, an extremely thoughtful and grounded person, Arun couldn’t have taken such a hurried decision!

“Yyy Yes! But can I get some time to think about it?” She gulped, to buy some time to digest what was happening to her life.

We are so conditioned to struggles as a way of living! That is why when the opportunities are given on a platter, there is a desire to pinch and check if it is a dream or a crude joke.

"Tell me now. Yes, or no?" Sarah had never seen Arun so impatient. "Yes!" "Actually, Arun, the concept of marriage is not yet on my radar." Arun stopped breathing. He did not know what was coming next.

"But I love you. I love you very much. And I don't want to lose you. If marriage is the only way in which we can be together,... So be it."

"Sarah, you want to get married out of fear of losing me. I see a risk of losing you if I get married to you.... But this is not the time for arguments. I guess the situation demands that we get married soon.

One can write an encyclopedia on reasons for which people get married........

Usually the reason is an 'urge' arising out of some sort of lack or an escape from something.

Little does one realize that ***life takes a full circle and brings one back to the starting point.***

If one begins one's married life with a feeling of a void, after a temporary gratification the void will still remain unfulfilled. Frustration sets in, if they feel that the investment was too steep against unpredictable returns.

If they get married to avoid being lonely, very soon loneliness will chase them.

If they get married to have more money in order to escape the feeling of paucity of wealth, very soon they will find themselves seeking still more.

If they get married to someone hoping to raise their social standard in order to avoid feeling low about themselves, they will definitely end up with experiences which make them feel like outsiders and 'low' amongst the elite society of their in-laws.

Those who get married to share something, come from a sense of abundance and end up experiencing more abundance.

Sarah tried inviting her father and mother but they did not respond with enthusiasm. Both of them sent their blessings and invited the couple to the USA.

Arun had invited some of his close relatives and friends for the wedding. Dipti maintained a cheerful demeanor to not let any of her relatives know of her displeasure. But deep in her heart, she was petrified about losing her brother, the only working relationship she'd had in her life so far.

The newly married couple went for a short holiday to a beautiful spa resort in the Maldives.

Arun had booked a lovely villa facing the ocean. They sat outside their villa in a king size beach recliner, generously lined with foam and covered with velvet. The effect of the warm sun bath and the rhythmic sounds of the ocean waves made them feel totally relaxed. Clad in bare minimum, they enjoyed the warm and humid weather.

Life is very boring if everything is hunky dory. And that's why we keep looking out for ways and means to get into trouble, when everything in life is going just perfectly fine.

Sarah was one of them. She could have chosen to extend this experience of serenity in Arun's arms, but no, she had to enjoy some challenges in order to make her life interesting.

"Arun, I can't believe I am married to someone who hasn't even said 'I love you' to me." She hoped he wouldn't dampen her mood this time by denying his love.

Arun went closer to her and put his arm around her. Sarah wanted something more than that of course.

"I love you," Arun's fingers affectionately held her shoulders as he whispered in her ears the three most enchanting words.

"Why did you not say so before?" Sarah choked as pearls of joy involuntarily spilled from her eyes.

"Because I am not sure what love is! I think ***love is the most misunderstood word by people in this world.*** He continued preaching as the philosopher in him took over. ***"Even those who claim to be talking about unconditional love have a condition of unconditionality!"*** For a while he got lost looking into infinity, as if he was trying to look beyond the horizon to discover something new today. Arun was intently analyzing his previous stints with love.

"For Dipti, love is all about possessiveness; for Ramu Chacha, love is all about loyalty; to my Mom, love meant sacrifice; to my Dad, love was all about giving security to someone." His mind was exploring his past relationships as he continued his monologue. Suddenly he became aware of Sarah's presence.

"What is love for you, Sarah?"

"Difficult question Arun. I never thought about it so far" averting her eyes as she attempted her reply.

"There was a time I hated everyone. I hated my father, I hated my mother for leaving me and I hated all my boyfriends, who made me feel used. Having been at the farm under your supervision and care, today if you ask me, I don't hate anyone. Not even my parents, who did not care to participate in the wedding of their only daughter. I don't feel hurt by their behavior anymore."

Sarah changed her position on the recliner to turn towards Arun. "I simply don't expect anything from anyone anymore."

"Not even from me?" Arun asked.

"No. You have given me so much in life, even if we have to part tomorrow, I will leave feeling totally complete. You have taught me to take each day as it comes. I have lived with you as if tomorrow would never come." She paused to reflect.

"Today, I am not worried about tomorrow. ***If you were taken care of in the past, there is no reason why you will not be taken care of in the future.***"

All this while, it was Arun who guided her, now it was she who was throwing light on love. Arun listened to her as she continued talking to him, leaning on him and her hands gently rubbing his palms.

Arun too had a choice of continuing to bask in that magical moment, but he had to probe deeper.

"Sarah, do you ever feel uneasy about what happened between your father and you?" Arun was slightly cautious. He knew the folly of talking about the past on a special evening like this, but he could not resist asking her.

"I did feel horrible about letting myself get sexually intimate with my dad, Arun. It took time to even accept that. Initially, all I knew was that girls are not supposed to have a sexual relationship with their fathers, but the desire to be physically close to a man was too overpowering. He was the only man in my life when I was in my teens. I looked overweight and chubby and not a single boy in my class wanted to date me." Her eyes looked defused as her mind drifted back into her past.

"Later, I worked hard to look like other girls, slim and in good shape. Gradually, my level of confidence started rising. I started dating. I realized that I was capable of attracting quite a few handsome guys and then I found no need to sleep with my Dad."

Arun kept staring at the changing colors in the sky as the sun was just about to set, periodically responding in soft monosyllables to let her know that he was indeed listening to her.

"Sounds selfish, doesn't it?" Sarah continued. "But that's how I was in the past. Rather than taking responsibility for my actions, I started blaming my father for leading me into the act. I was full of anger."

Sarah paused to reflect on her past life. She suddenly got an insight on why she was so angry with her father. "Perhaps, I used anger as a defense mechanism to mask my guilt and shame. When I managed to resolve the anger, I started feeling ashamed of myself. That's when I did not want to show my face to the world. I felt ashamed of sleeping with my Dad!"

Anger is a very powerful but destructive weapon we use to defend ourselves from unacceptable emotions like helplessness, powerlessness, frustration, guilt, shame, embarrassment, and a sense of weakness.

"Not only did I sleep with my father, I also took advantage of him.

I used my body to get material benefits. I felt like a whore, Arun," her voice changed as overwhelming emotions choked her vocal cord. Arun almost regretted touching her sore spot but it had to reach its logical conclusion.

"Are you still angry with your father?"

"No, not for sleeping with me. I felt used. Yet I have almost resolved that part of my life. What I am still angry about is that he pretended to be faithful to me... and then he got married to some other woman."

"Did he ever say that you are the only woman in his life?"

"No, he never said that." "He always claimed that he had dedicated his life to only one woman and that was me."

"How did you feel when you heard about his marriage?"

felt betrayed. Horribly cheated..."

"Who betrayed whom, Sarah?"

"He betrayed me, Arun."

"Really?" Arun leaned over her to look deep in her eyes.

As if he wanted to show her a mirror.

The eyes of the people around you are the greatest reflectors of who you are. If ever you care to find out who you are, simply gaze into their eyes and allow the honest picture to emerge.

"Yes, you are right. First, I betrayed him. I walked out of his life first. But I came here in search of a guru."

"Did you not leave him temporarily for other boys?"

"Yes, I can imagine, he must have felt so much pain. He was so possessive about me."

"Did you ever think of getting married to him?"

"No. However advanced the western society is, it is not yet open enough to accept a father and a daughter's marriage."

She kept quiet. Arun being a good listener, gave her a lot of time to introspect in between their conversation.

"In fact, some of the ancient tribes are more liberal, they have no rules." She took one more deep breath.

"Arun, tell me, did I do anything wrong by sleeping with my father?"

The lover in him was about to get judgmental. A part of him wanted to blame that bastard for misleading his innocent daughter in an outright incestuous relationship.

We always like to blame others for what happens to our loved ones.

He realized that he was playing the same blame game as Dipti was, vis-a-vis him and Sarah. He gracefully admitted to himself.

"From the higher perspective, there is nothing right and nothing wrong. There are only actions and their consequences."

He gave her some time to digest what he had just said.

"If you do something that you are uneasy with or feel guilty about, you start subconsciously punishing yourself for doing so. You don't allow yourself to be happy. You don't allow yourself to thrive in life."

There is no greater enemy than guilt. Guilt is the most destructive emotion that humans ever harbored.

"I thought it was required in order to be well behaved. I felt very proud of feeling guilty once upon a time. If I didn't have the feeling of guilt, I would have harmed so many people."

"And if you feel guilty, you tend to harm yourself." "That is all right," Sarah interrupted impatiently. "Why is that all right?" "It is all right to harm yourself but not others." "Sarah, tell me, you do believe in God, don't you?" "Yes, very much."

"Let us presume that God exists. What is the greatest gift that God has given you?"

"My body? My mind? My personality? My 'SELF'!"

"Exactly, the greatest gift we receive as humans is the "self." "Imagine if you had given a gift to someone and if that gift is handled with harshness, would you like it?" he argued like a seasoned debater. "What right do you have to punish, harm and mishandle the greatest gift you have got from God? That gift is you."

Arun knew these were fresh insights for Sarah. He changed his position and leaned back on the beach chair, leaving Sarah in his arms to ruminate over what he had said.

Sarah kept watching the waves washing away the footprints of birds walking on the loose wet sand. She suddenly felt as if all her past ideas, beliefs and conditioning were suddenly getting washed away with these new perspectives.

By and large, we have more expectations from ourselves than we have from others. That is why it is so easy to forgive others but it is very difficult to forgive our own selves.

Behind a transparent veil of tears, Sarah slipped into a deep introspective mood...

Sarah had done a lot of work on herself. She had managed to forgive herself to an extent, but she still found it very difficult to locate all the aspects that needed her forgiveness.

Both of them remained quiet for the rest of the evening, but in their minds, they kept chatting with each other at different wavelengths all throughout.

It was a different experience for both of them.

Sarah had read somewhere that ***when people are in love with each other they don't need to use words to communicate. As the emotional distance increases between people, the volume of verbal communication goes higher. Eventually, with a broken cord of love, people resort to shouting and screaming and yet fail to communicate what they want to communicate.***

They walked back towards the bar and selected a cozy corner for themselves. Sarah ordered a sweet lime soda for herself and looked at Arun, waiting for him to order something from the wine menu. He did not bother to even look at it and instead said, "Make that two."

Sarah gave him a look of surprise. "Sarah, first of all, I need to handle the intoxication of your presence." "What? I don't believe this. You? With this Hindi film dialogue?" Sarah was amused.

"You're responsible for all that, Sarah!"

The dinner was served in an isolated tent with lovely chiffon curtains, giving them adequate privacy and yet enabling them to enjoy the presence of the vast ocean in front of them. The raised platform was lined with a Kashmiri carpet. A butler, silently waiting at a distance, was assigned exclusively for their service.

"Do you know Sarah, that I am quite afraid of love?" Sarah looked at him with a lot of love in the dim candlelight.

"Yes, I know it." "You knew it?"

"Yes, it's very obvious when you interact with people around you. Though I haven't seen you interacting with too many of them, but with whatever little glimpses I've had of you, I felt it strongly."

"How? I mean what did you observe?" Arun didn't try hiding his puzzled feelings.

"I feel that ***those who are scared of love create a barrier between themselves and the world.*** They appear unapproachable. Not because they don't want to be approached, but because they are scared of getting very close to someone and getting hurt in the bargain. They make it difficult for people to love them, putting too many conditions, too many expectations and too many obstacles; they behave, at times, absolutely unpredictably. The moment a person seems to come emotionally close, they get into a 'flight' mode." Sarah continued staring at the flickering candle flame as she whispered her gospel.

She might have continued expounding had Arun not interrupted her by calling the butler inside the tent to order his double malt Scotch whisky on the rocks.

There was a long silence after the butler left.

Sarah chose to give him some space. She saw that she had lectured him too much. Arun was having a hard time facing these disclosures.

"I did that with you Sarah, several times. There were times when I left the farmhouse for days together. I went not because I had any urgent business, but because I wanted to avoid seeing you."

"I was aware about that, somewhere, " She took her eyes off the flame to look at him with a lot of reassurance and love.

"Did you not hate me for that? On one hand, I was advising you on why you should not be running away and on the other hand, I was displaying the same weakness."

Before Sarah could answer, the butler was back with an entire bottle of whisky and an ice pail. He put a lot of ice cubes in the glass and poured the whisky over as guided by Arun.

Sarah waited for him to take a sip. But he guzzled the entire glass even before the butler could leave the tent. Without waiting for the butler, he prepared another peg for himself.

"Running away is a survival mechanism, Arun, to save ourselves. If you thought by running away from me meant saving yourself, it's only natural to do that, isn't it? At times it is almost imperative."

Sarah quietly watched him emptying another peg into his disturbed guts. There was an awkward silence between them for a long time. Perhaps Arun was waiting for the much-needed whisky to take over his disturbed psyche.

The escape measures taken to evade the feelings of guilt often set up fertile ground to germinate more guilt.

To silence his conscience from the guilt of having escaped life, he was now escaping under the cover of alcohol.

He stretched out his tired body on a soft mattress. His head rested on Sarah's beautiful legs. A part of him wanted to stop this serious talk and simply play with her breasts.

Sarah loved to have his head on her lap. She kept moving her fingers through his soft, thick, curly locks with a lot of love and gentleness.

"The question is, why are you so scared of emotional intimacy? Have you been hurt in the past?"

Arun knew this question was coming. In his own way he was preparing himself to expose the old wounds. He had been avoiding this confrontation for a long time.

He kept his glass of whisky on a carved wooden counter in the center of the tent, slightly raised his upper body to move even closer to her, putting both his hands around her neck, he courageously opened his mouth to answer this difficult question. "Yes, I never told you about it. This was way back, when I was 25 years old. Annie left me for someone else.

She was the last person in my life who has been able to hurt me so deeply. No, Dipti too hurt me when she could not accept you, but I can forgive her because I know her very well. She is so possessive about me that it is natural that she would behave like she did."

Sarah raised her legs slightly and adjusted a cushion to support her propped up upper body. Her fingers moved as if disentangling hair on his head and chest. It appeared so metaphorical, was she disentangling the hair or the issues buried in his head and heart?

"Tell me about Annie."

"It's a closed chapter. Let us not talk about it anymore. She is no more a part of my life." Arun tried getting up to go back to their villa, but could not, as she refused to budge from her position.

Instead, she prepared another peg for him and handed over the glass to him.

"Does she affect you?" "Not anymore."

"Mr. Arun Deshmukh! I hear a lie from you for the first time."

She compassionately tried searching for the answers in Arun's eyes.

When you cannot get information verbally, try extracting it through the eyes.

"Sarah, please don't spoil this great day for us. I want to forget everything about it forever. Will you help me to do that? Please?"

"Of course, Arun."

That night he knocked himself out with whisky. His behavior stunned her. Sarah had to support and escort him to their villa at the beach. It turned out to be quite an embarrassing scene. Once inside the villa, he started crying aloud inconsolably.

Why do people change overnight once they get married, Sarah wondered. Probably ***the marriage license gives people the security to drop their pretense.***

Often getting married is like winning a coveted challenge in the game of life. They feel triumphant but act placid. Their spouse feels like a trophy in their pocket.

That night Arun was a different person in bed. He kept uttering Annie's name throughout the night. He almost forced a reluctant Sarah to succumb to his beastly lust. Sarah sincerely regretted not getting drunk along with him.

The following day he got up with a severe headache, late in the morning. He apologized to her for getting drunk. Sarah managed to remain calm. She had seen her dad doing the same. She had felt her dad's pain when her mom had left him. He never cried but the pain used to show up frequently.

Sarah had a lot of time to brood in the morning over what had happened. She could not stop comparing Arun with her father. How could she have attracted this dad-like behavior from a man who had never even met her dad ever?

All this while she believed that she had resolved her past with her dad, but no! When Arun accidentally triggered the buried pains of the past, she realized some spots in her heart were still sore and raw.

Her father too had probably used her to fill up the void that her mom had left behind. And now Arun was doing the same!

Sarah started losing her emotional balance. The train of negative thoughts kept taking her back to the unresolved past.

The number of emotional breakdowns is directly proportional to unresolved past unpleasant events. If you are looking at remaining in emotional balance all the time, it is important that you resolve your past issues effectively and appropriately. Sarah had managed to resolve a lot from her past but the feeling of being used was yet to be handled effectively.

Oh, no. I can't handle this anymore. I can't allow this to happen to me anymore!

Sometimes the fight to make the miniscule pain oblivious becomes so huge, that it seems foolish to an onlooker. But the fighter continues to put in all his energies, unable to see that truth....

An emotionally disturbed mind is like boiling water. It cannot reflect the truth/answers lying in the deeper layers.

I wish I could terminate this relationship. He should have told me about Annie before getting married. He never mentioned a word...

As if I have told him everything about what happened between Dad and me... Quickly she argued with herself. I did not tell him because it is very painful. Can it be that Arun did not tell me because it was painful for him? Doesn't matter, whatever it is, I just want to know how to stop being in pain.

I don't want to keep being the surrogate for other people all my life...

If you do not know how to handle your thoughts and feelings, you can very well ruin a perfectly pleasurable relationship or even an occasion. Sarah and Arun were hell-bent on ruining their holiday anyway. Arun noticed the coldness in her behavior but did not have the guts to ask what happened. He was definite that in a drunken state he had blurted something to offend her.

The indifference continued even after they were back. Arun had washed his hands off the farmhouse and was busy trying to establish a new business for himself. He was busy getting in touch with his old contacts to find out the possibility of doing so.

Sarah was busy turning the house around from a bachelor pad to a family 'home'.

Something inside her heart was hurting and the same was with Arun. He avoided spending time with her. He would leave the house early and come back only when he was very tired or completely drunk.

Sitting all alone in an unknown house in an unknown city was getting Sarah frustrated.

Sarah, as usual, pretended to sleep when Arun arrived late at night, totally drunk, and Ramu Chacha would open the door. Sometimes when he did not drink, and he opened the door with his own set of house keys, he would collapse into bed next to Sarah.

This went on for three weeks.

On one such fateful night, Sarah pretended to be asleep as usual, but his noisy behavior and loud calling of Annie's name kept her awake.

Arun practically threw his drunken body on the bed carelessly with his head resting on her breasts. His hands started exploring ways to unbutton her nightgown. Sarah got up to leave the room but he held her tight. In a rage he tore her nightgown.

Sarah had been repeatedly subjected to this kind of behavior before. Her father had become violent with her after she had started ignoring him because of her young boyfriends.

Her refusal had been interpreted as arrogance by her father. He would often try to break her pride by forcing her in bed or showing off his supremacy of being the dominant player.

Sarah had reluctantly complied with him for his money. This went on until her mother intervened and advised her to lodge a complaint with the police.

The pattern broke when, as a settlement, her father agreed to shift her to another apartment and give her a monthly allowance.

Sarah, in her new apartment, got her freedom and money; along with plenty of loneliness. Initially, she felt used by her father, later she received the same treatment from her boyfriends.

When she refused to go to bed with them, they stopped seeing her. No amount of alcohol or smoke would fill up the void that she was experiencing.

She wanted a man who loved her and not because he needed her.

She had heard that love should be free of need. She wondered if she would ever experience that kind of love.

Sarah had been very happy to get Arun. She thought she was the one who needed him more than he needed her. Soon she realized that she was actually only filling up the deep void in his heart.

Oh God! Why could I not have found this out before marrying him? Why did he have to get drunk and only then bring up his weaknesses? She thought she could trust him, but it was her misfortune that this side of Arun had remained unknown to her until now.

Sarah felt cheated, let down, and thoroughly used.

A part of her tried using logic, but in vain.

They say that history repeats itself and that's what happened to her.

It is interesting how life goes a full circle. We tend to attract similar kinds of experiences periodically.

When she used to have problems, she used to turn to Arun. Now she had a problem with Arun, whom could she turn to?

Of course, to Arun's sagacity.

Whenever you are faced with problems, just think of the good days and think of what made the days so good. You will probably get a clue on how to bloom in gloom.

She started remembering her good old days at the farm. She started recalling Arun's teaching.

The first thing that came to her mind was his explanation about being in the now.

"You seldom suffer because of what is happening in the now. You suffer when what is happening in the now reminds you of the discomfort of the past or makes you worry about the future." She remembered his words as she opened a diary that she used to write in at the farmhouse.

All right, she began her analysis, *actually the problem is because I am worried, worried about my future with him and I am responding to him out of my past backlog. If I did not have a past backlog of being used by my father, I would not have behaved like I did. I would not have felt used the way I am feeling now.*

The universe gives you multiple opportunities to test your abilities to come out with empowering responses to life.

It should not upset me that Arun has not been able to overcome the void left behind by Annie. It is my shortcoming that I haven't been able to accept him unconditionally and give him that kind of love and anchoring which can fill up the void in his heart.

She started flipping through her diary, and went through her notes on Arun's commentary during her farmhouse days... ***You are on the path of an empowered life when you take total responsibility for everything that is happening around you and stop blaming others for what is happening to you.***

I need to understand and accept the ground reality. I am behaving with indifference to him, because I want to escape from the situation rather than accept and face the situation head on with grace.

She remembered him talking in detail once about the role that women and men play in a family unit. It was an interesting conversation they'd had sitting on the swing of their farmhouse.

"The nature of man is to be a provider, a protector, an aggressive being, a go-getter in life. When he chooses to be passive, and laid back, he invites troubles for himself, unless he partners with a woman who has more masculine attributes to her personality."

"What is the feminine role?" Sarah had asked.

"Feminine energy is the one which grounds, which nurtures, one which needs to be protected, and to be taken care of, that which is like an anchor for her male counterpart. She is like a magnet, who can remain still, passive and yet attract movement towards her. She is the receiver in life."

"A lot of men and women these days don't want to play the roles assigned to them. They then go through the resultant physiological disturbances."

I did not quite agree with what he had said, he had sounded too orthodox in his opinion, but let me try it out. Maybe if I did play the role of being an anchor, would I be able to undo the damage between the two of us?

Another important thing that he had once said was that ***those who have the fear of being controlled, land up becoming control freaks themselves. Those who have the fear of being***

overpowered, never miss a chance to display their power to others.

By refusing to have sex with him, am I demonstrating my feminine dominance to him? And is that why he is responding with more dominance? Well, we are going nowhere. Let me stop this game; let me drop my belief of being used; let me put aside my demands of undivided attention from him; let me try accepting him, including his past, neutrally with all the love I can generate for him.

What if he rejects my love? The little monkey in her mind questioned her.

We always have these little voices inside us that keep arguing with us. We have to shut them up sometimes or keep them occupied with some mundane jobs, so that we can focus on something that is necessary.

Sarah spent that day at the beauty salon. She changed her hairstyle, bought a nice perfume, bought a few candles for the house, she also changed the bed spread to a lovely, embroidered silk one.

She purchased a smart night suit for him and a light lilac colored robe with pretty lace work for herself.

At 10 o'clock that night, she called him to find out where he was.

He sounded drunk but seemed happy to hear her voice. She had almost broken the habit of calling him up to find out where he was and at what time he'd be coming home. More often than not he would have his business dinner and come back home late, fully or quite drunk.

Today Arun was pleased to receive Sarah's call of concerned inquiry. Though he was drunk, the excitement made him listen to her as alertly as he could.

"What are you doing, darling?" He asked. His voice was filled with love. "I am waiting for you, Arun."

"What did you do the whole day today?" He wanted to keep the conversation rolling in spite of the loud music playing at the pub.

"I shopped to give you a surprise in the evening." Arun was about to ask what the surprise was but thought it would be silly. "What did you do today, Arun?" "I waited for your call, Sarah." He sounded very sincere.

Sarah reddened. She felt ashamed of herself. Unknowingly, perhaps she had hurt him so much.

"Please come home soon." "I'll be there in ten minutes, darling."

He did not take out the house keys to open the door. He rang the bell, waiting with the hope to see his lovely wife greet him. She opened the door and gave him a tight hug. "WELCOME HOME, Honey!"

"I do feel at home but only in your arms, Sarah. Don't ever be so indifferent again, it almost destroyed me."

"I am sorry."

"Sorry again?" Both of them laughed.

They had a great time dining, with light music, the lovely fragrance of aromatic candles lit in the background and a yummy blueberry cheesecake to top it up.

"You changed your hairstyle?" "Yes, do you like it?"

"You always look good to me but yes, it suits you a lot. It's giving your face a much softer look."

Sarah felt amused and wondered if it really was the new hairstyle or something else that was responsible for this soft feel?

He helped her take the dishes to the kitchen. "Where is Ramu Chacha?"

I gave him a day off to visit some friends. He had been asking for it for quite some time. I thought today was the perfect occasion to do that!

"Umm! Smart."

He settled down on the sofa with the remote in his hand flipping the channels.

Normally, Sarah would be very upset with this act. For her, this was a sure shot rejection. She had spent the whole day shopping to make this evening a great one for both of them and had waited the entire day to spend some time with him. She had even given the day off to Ramu Chacha so that they could spend uninterrupted time together. But she forgot one thing...

"I wish I had cut off the TV cable connection today," she told him as she slipped next to him on the sofa.

He switched off the TV and kept the remote aside. Putting one of his arms around her shoulders with a lot of warmth he said, "Nothing is more important than you," while caressing her cheek with the other hand.

"Do you still love me?" Sarah wanted to keep the conversation going. "Do I have a choice? I tried to be indifferent to you and I have tried being detached from you. I just couldn't...! There is something about you, and I can't understand even with my freaking logical mind, what keeps bringing me back to you."

He leaned over her, placing his lips on hers. Suddenly, his lips were moving all over her face, slowly moving lower...tracing her soft sensuous body.

She felt as if she was melting in his arms. Her arms started moving all over his body, as if exploring every pore of his very being.

Suddenly his attention went to her nightgown, "Very sexy!" "I have bought you something as well."

"Who cares about wearing anything when you are around?" he smiled, deepening the dimple on his cheek, and carried her in his arms to the bed.

Chapter Five

It was one of those busy mornings and as usual Arun was immersed in his morning routine. He was very faithful to his yoga, his newspaper, his breakfast of juice and sprouts with yoghurt. Sarah waited for an opportunity to grab his attention and found one as he was shaving in the bathroom.

"I would like to come to your office starting tomorrow." "Why?" asked Arun, "Not that I mind, but what made you think of this?" "Arun, previously there was a great desire to be just a simple homemaker, to manage the house for someone I love, to cook for him, to do everything for him. I felt great when you allowed me to have that experience, but now this life has lost its charm. It has become mundane."

Arun opted to play the good listener by not interfering or judging her before she had completed her narration totally.

"You are busy the whole day and I feel so bored and at times worthless. I don't want to live this kind of life anymore."

At every point of time, we have a choice of being either content or discontented. Perhaps we choose to be discontented out of fear of stagnation in life.

"You think you will feel less bored if you come to my office? What will you do in the office?"

"I will do whatever you ask me to do."

"Do you think that will make you feel more worthy or significant?" "Probably, not."

"Let me explain something to you Sarah. Many times, ***we create the whole drama of life because we want to avoid a certain experience. Interestingly, at the end of the whole drama we face exactly the same feeling that we were trying to escape from. If we are not vigilant enough, life will continue moving in loops.***"

"I did not get you. Can you explain that to me again?"

"I would love to have you around at the office every day. But that will not meet your need."

"Because currently your need is to feel good about yourself. You have stopped feeling good about just being a homemaker, because millions of women have been doing it anyway. What was earlier a fascinating experience does not excite you anymore."

She had tears in her eyes. "Thanks, Arun, for understanding me so well, but that is not the answer to my situation right now."

"Sarah, I am with you in anything that you choose for yourself in life. But since you are starting something afresh, I want you to be precise and careful about the seed you sow."

"Seed?"

"You know, Sarah, our mind is like a fertile ground. Our thoughts are like seeds and our life is like a tree. The tree may appear different from the seed that you have sown... but invariably yields the same kind of seeds in multiples."

"I still don't quite get you, Arun."

"Do you agree that we all play games in life?" "Yes."

"Do you agree there is a reason why we play these games?"

"I agree, but I don't understand the reasons other than boredom." "Boredom is the commonest reason and provides a fertile ground for the tree of life-games to grow."

Arun had finished his shave but chose to continue the conversation.

"We play the game to demonstrate what we are not."

"OK..." This was Sarah's unique style of keeping a conversation going. "If someone feels useless for some reason, that person will play the game of being useful in life. If someone feels poor, he will play the game of being the wealthy one. If the feeling is of failure, the game of being successful will be a good challenge. We are all busy playing some game or the other." "I understand what you are trying to tell me, but I don't really agree. I fail to see what game I play?"

"***Your subjectivity will not let you understand your subtle games***," said Arun as he splashed on some aftershave.

"What do you mean by subjectivity?" Sarah though perplexed was getting a bit impatient.

He had a small mirror in the bathroom. He held it extremely close to Sarah's face; almost touching her nose. "Can you see your face clearly?"

"Just take it slightly back please?"

"That's exactly what I am telling you. It is difficult to be your own observer at times, because you see yourself from a very close angle and you lose objectivity."

Sarah's stubbornness refused to buy his philosophy. She thought Arun was trying to dissuade her from coming to office and that was why he was taking the conversation to another track.

She was not prepared to listen to his preaching. All she wanted to hear was either a "Yes" or a "No".

Arun excused himself and vanished behind the pearl white shower curtain.

Sarah took a deep breath and went to the kitchen.

Sarah felt incomplete and doubted whether Arun would like to continue the conversation after this interruption, but to her great surprise, he started explaining once again as he settled for breakfast. He had never tried so hard to explain something to Sarah. But today, he was persistent about reaching out to her with his philosophy.

"I know, Sarah, you are impatient with me," as he metaphorically cracked the shell of a half-boiled egg gently.

"I am sorry, but I am too bored just being at home, watching TV, shopping, visiting the beauty salon and cooking in the evening. I need something more in life."

No matter what is spoken to us, we listen according to our own previous conditioning.

"I am losing the purpose of life," Sarah tried explaining.

"Come back to me with an appropriate purpose and we will discuss this in the evening," Arun said, sprinkling the salt.

"My purpose is to find a purpose," Sarah muttered with a long sigh.

"That's right. Coming to the office just to beat the boredom is not the way to find your purpose in life," Arun said, pretending to be in a hurry to leave.

She was angry but tried hiding it from Arun. He still had the egg on his plate.

"Do you know what this is?" "An egg."

"If it had been fertilized, what would have become of it?"

"A hen or a cock?" Sarah felt like a small child being taught by a doting father.

"And eventually what would it have given birth to?" "Again, an egg."

"That's what I am trying to tell you. Life keeps moving in a circle. If you plant a mango seed, obviously the tree will yield mangoes and not coconuts."

"This is common sense, Arun, but you are going round and round in circles and I am not getting your point!"

It is most irritating when you are forced to listen to something you are not prepared for.

"If you take up anything in life to avoid getting bored, eventually you will end up getting bored." Arun finally summarized, noticing Sara's obvious irritation surface up.

Life takes a full circle. When you start your journey to avoid certain feelings, more often than not you land up experiencing what you wanted to avoid.

He picked up his briefcase and gave her a hug before leaving the house. Sarah was in no mood to go anywhere today. She started clearing up the dining table with Ramu Chacha's help. She knew that Arun was right somehow. But what he said did not make any sense to her. Or rather, the adamant child in her did not want to make any sense of what was discussed in the morning.

A beep on her mobile phone broke her trail of thoughts. She had received a text from Arun.

"You have all your answers."

This is weird. She marveled at the synchronicity of the event. She was just thinking of meditating to arrive at the answers.

She sat quietly on her bed and closed her eyes. She asked herself, *What is it that I want?*

The answer was quick and short....... *I want to prove something to myself.* After a little pause she put another question to herself.

Why do I need to prove something to myself? And there came from within, a quick answer once again. *Because I am feeling insignificant.*

All right, so what I don't want is a feeling of being insignificant.

Now it is making some sense to me. In my entire life whenever I felt insignificant, I tried doing something to counter that, but I still could not overcome that feeling.

Whenever I felt used by my father, I felt insignificant.

When I tried throwing my weight around him, he stopped asking for sexual favors, making me feel even more insignificant.

Every time I tried to attract a guy and behaved like a tease, he left me before I could leave him, perpetuating the same feeling.

The last straw was my father getting married without even informing me.

Was this his way of proving that I am insignificant in his life?

I held back sexually from Arun and he responded by getting more involved in his business matters, which further endorsed the feeling.

Even his sister succeeded in making me feel small.

Thank God, I could not find a guru in India or else I would have found one more way to endorse this damn belief!

Is it my Ego? Is it wrong to desire significance?

Oh! too many questions. I wish Arun comes home early today. I can't wait to see him.

She could not keep her eyes closed and meditate. A sudden ring of the doorbell distracted her already disturbed mind.

She opened the door to find Arun. "Arun? At this time of the day?"

"Sorry Sarah, I forgot my handkerchief. Can you get one from the wardrobe?"

She went inside the bedroom but returned empty handed.

"Arun, can you stay back at home and not go to work today? I have something very important to talk to you about.

"So, you are planning to bore me with your issue of boredom?" Even though he was just teasing her, she felt hurt and offended.

"Arun, you know it is not boredom. It is much more than that. I need you today to hold the mirror far away from me, so that I can see the answers for myself," Sarah spoke, overcoming a great resistance from her stiffened vocal cords.

Arun dropped his office bag on the sofa and put his arm around her. "I am sure this day will be a very fruitful day."

Sarah went closer to him to help him loosen his necktie. She helped him undress and get into his shorts and T-shirt.

As she was putting his clothes in the laundry, she found a handkerchief while emptying his trouser pocket. He looked at her sheepishly like a naughty child.

"Do you need to give me a reason to come back home?" "No. Nno,.. perhaps, yes."

He smiled. She smiled too as both of them settled down with a cup of coffee on their relaxing couch in front of the terrace swimming pool.

"It feels nice to be at home at this time, especially on a working day." Arun stretched out, his body unwinding completely.

"I am equally thrilled with this pleasant surprise. Thanks, Arun. You have made my day."

"It does feel wonderful to have you here with me on this beautiful sunny day."

"Tell me, where do we start? Where is my mirror?" "Look into the swimming pool. You will be able to see yourself very well."

Arun tried some humor with her.

"It's too shallow. I prefer looking into your eyes. I haven't found anything deeper than that."

"Hey! You can't steal my dialogue!" Arun was in a mischievous mood, willing to have a little fun. "C'mon, I wanted to say that to you."

But Sarah was serious. She refused to get distracted by Arun's subtle jokes. "I mean it. Tell me what do your eyes see me as?"

"Why does it matter to you?" said Arun, seriously realizing that Sarah was not willing to make light of the conversation.

"It matters because you are the most important person in my life." "Important? Hmm. Think again. Who is the most important person in your life? Tell me?"

"You, of course. Any doubts?" "Not at all," Arun said emphatically even as he was relaxing in his chair. "May I take the risk of asking you, who is the most important person in your life.

"You have taken a big risk baby.... because you know I don't lie."

Sarah paused her breathing awaiting his response.

"The most important person in my life is ME."

"I have learnt it the hard way, Sarah, you will learn it too. Hope you don't go through the pain I went through in discovering that."

"Every time I felt rejected by someone, I would go through pain. I would convince myself that I am not important enough for that person and that's why I was rejected," Arun continued.

"That is why it took such a long time for me to tell you that I love you."

Rejection is one of the most painful emotions. ***People prefer rejecting so many precious opportunities in life in order to avoid the pain of being rejected by others.***

"It is interesting! I also felt the same way when my mother chose the other guy over me. I am sure my dad must have felt the same way too."

"That is why it felt so good to be needed and sometimes there is a desire of being a guru figure in the future. Feeling important, you see," Sarah smirked at her own silly logic of the past.

"When I gave you the job of a gardener, how did you feel?"

"Wretched! I had just got the news of my father's second marriage. I was so hurt... and feeling very insecure about my survival. I did not know whether he would sponsor my return to the USA.

I was not sure if he would ever give me any money...ever. His surprise move left me clueless about his next step. The future appeared bleak.

The best-known fear is the fear of the unknown.

Sarah took a long pause while Arun waited patiently for her to continue. "I didn't have any accommodation, or money for food. I had no choice, Arun, so I took up your offer. But I accepted it as God's grace eventually."

She loved chatting with Arun. He could turn even the most ordinary conversation into a special experience, which invariably resulted in some deep insights.

"But what I didn't really understand is why on earth did you assign me that particular job? I was not an expert gardener anyway and there were many other ways in which you could have absorbed me. I was ready to do anything for you. Anything, you know that" she grinned cheekily.

Arun changed his position to get closer to her. "When I saw you for the first time, my first impression was that, in search of spirituality, somewhere you had lost touch with your ground reality. It was important for you to get grounded and enjoy the process of survival...back to basics, you see......."

"Why a gardening job?" Sarah interrupted impatiently.

"Working with mud and sand is the best way to get grounded. All that you do throughout the day is take care of the basic process of life. Giving food, water and shelter to the saplings, nurturing, caring, and helping plants survive the initial few days until they become strong enough to be on their own."

How metaphorical! she thought. Sarah's mind went back to the fields, the heat of the sun, rough soil under her feet, dry roti with a chilli and onion for meals.........absolutely basic............ but I managed to survive. Not only survive, I managed to thrive.........She felt overwhelmed by Arun's role in her life......... He had actually taught her how to live her life..............with zest, to survive and thrive.......

Everyone survives until the time they die. Only those who live their lives fully know how to thrive, rather than merely survive.

"You were nurturing me as I was nurturing the plants in your fields."

"No, Sarah. You were nurturing yourself. Did you realize you started eating well, you started sleeping well? You were no longer constantly lost in your thoughts."

"Those were the best days of my life, Arun. Except that I missed you.

I would daily wish to have a glimpse of you. And the day you would come to the fields, I would feel so excited," Sarah suddenly looked like a baby.

"Did you know I used to come to the fields to see you most of the time? Of course, I needed to supervise, but seeing you was a major incentive to get out in the hot summer."

"Aaahaa! I wish I knew. You gave me the impression that you didn't care. I even considered the possibility of you being gay!"

"Ha, ha, ha!" Sarah's candidness made Arun roll over with laughter. His face turned red and tears started rolling down his cheeks. As he continued laughing, Sarah bit her lip. Finally, she too let out an embarrassed giggle.

"Really, you Americans! You land up labeling so easily! Actually, it is not your fault. When I refused to get married, even Dipti once asked me such a question."

Sarah was still embarrassed and wanted to change the topic of conversation.

"All right, I understood about the farming part, but what about the next promotion?" she said it with a twinkle in her eyes.

"I don't think you have yet understood my point of view,......." Arun was serious once again.

"We are spiritual beings who have chosen to go through physical experiences, called life."

"Our first commitment is to fulfil the soul's need, by honoring our basic existence, our survival. If we do not honor this and expect others including God to do so, we are evading the process of life."

"It is important to face the process of life head on and tell the universe, 'Yes! I am willing to survive. Not only to survive but to thrive in this material world'."

Arun, like a good teacher, was repeating this point to ensure that Sarah got the philosophy correctly.

"This step is so important! If we miss out on learning the correct attitude towards survival, we could come across serious complications in the later part of life."

"What kind of complications, Arun?"

"See, there is an animal in all of us. So, whenever we come across dangerous situations, we respond to it with 'fight' or 'flight'."

"What? Do we fight like animals? I don't think so," Sarah disagreed.

"A few of us do fight like animals, but we have modified and become sophisticated in our fight response. We do fight for our property. We fight for our rights. We fight for assets. We fight for so many things, sometimes in sophisticated ways, sometimes in not so sophisticated ways. How do we take flight? Very easy...when we give up, because we are neither able to fight nor resolve the situation, it becomes a kind of flight... we try to run away from difficult situations. We run away from conflict...we run away from facing challenges, even humiliation, emotional pains and what not."

"You said there are three ways."

"The third way is playing dead. When you realize you can neither fight nor run away and you can't even face it......... all you do is play dead. The milder form of playing dead is showing indifference and when there is a strong need to play dead, you manifest what is called depression."

"That is what I did for years, when I could not run away from my father and I could not even fight for myself," mused Sarah.

"I tried fighting with my dad and it didn't work out, so I tried escaping from him. Eventually I played dead to him."

A long pause and she started once again. "Did I do it for my survival?"

"You did it for effective survival as a human," Arun's voice was comforting and at the same time reassuring.

"Is it wrong to fight, take flight or play dead for your survival?" Sarah asked for deeper insight from her husband, philosopher and guide.

"No, it is not wrong. It is baseless. But we all survive till the time we are supposed to survive. It is not enough to survive alone. But do we get past surviving? The question is, do we thrive in life or not?"

"Wait a minute! This sounds more complicated now." Sarah wanted some more clarity like a good student. "What's the difference between surviving and thriving?"

"Even a comatose patient in the hospital bed can survive for years together, but he is not thriving in his life."

"Hmmm. I understand it now."

"We all live, but not all of us live 100% all the time. We all die once, but some of us kill ourselves several times in lame attempts to survive."

"Thriving is living your highest possible potential, being 100% of who you are, exploring all the facets of human existence."

Sarah raised her eyebrows in disbelief.

"Anything that we do against our own interest is like killing ourselves. It's called self-sabotage. So, many times when we are just about to do well in life, we cut ourselves off. Is it not slow suicide?"

Arun continued, "If we have missed out on the experience of thriving in childhood, as adults we become financially and materially very insecure. We miss out on the zest in life, we become self-sabotagers."

"Self-sabotagers?"

"Not having the desire to thrive in life leads us to acquire a suicidal attitude."

"I didn't have a suicidal tendency," Sarah respected Arun for his 'Gyan', but at this point it was difficult for her to accept this concept. Somehow, where this statement was concerned, she thought Arun was erring.

"You don't have to literally kill yourself to commit suicide. ***You are committing slow suicide by not living your life fully in any case.*** You fell in that category when I met you at the airport."

"You are so right. I was on a path that was detrimental to my growth until then. Something shifted when you put me on to field work at the farm. I began to enjoy what you called the process of survival. I started enjoying the dry rough 'roti' that I would get at the end of the day. I started enjoying sleeping on the cotton strapped bed, and yet got good sleep. Sometimes I would sleep on the floor because it would be too hot on the bed. In spite of that, I would sleep like a log and get up hungry the next day to eat some more 'Rotis'. It's hard to believe that I did it. But honestly, I had no complaints."

"You were upset when I put you on the job of pleasing me."

"I am so sorry! My mind was so conditioned then. My previous experiences of pleasing men the way they wanted me to please them were not so great. I was sickened by what I thought you expected."

"You felt afraid?" Arun wanted Sarah to continue talking.

"I didn't want to lose you in the bargain. I was not even afraid of sleeping with you or pleasing you in any way, but my past experiences taught me that men used me and left me. I didn't want history to repeat itself."

"So eventually, did you feel used by me too?"

"I tried hard not to let that feeling cripple my mind and body. By then I loved you too much to even think in those terms. I was ready to do whatever you asked. I was busy ensuring that I did not lose you. So, I complied with everything that you asked of me. In the bargain, I started enjoying the small little pleasurable moments of life. The seeker in me felt very guilty for that indulgence and I did go through some conflict periodically. But thanks to your help and guidance, I started discovering God in the beauty of life. Thank you so much, Arun, for that."

"That was your second lesson, Sarah, to enjoy life for yourself and make life enjoyable for others. Try pleasing yourself and others for the sake of pleasing and feel the joy you get out of the process. And, when I say pleasing, it is not only the act of sex. You could please somebody by your smile, your touch, with a lovely fragrance, with flowers. There are so many ways to spread joy and beauty."

"If that's the case, then why have people created so much hype about sex?

There is so much pain and pleasure associated with the process of sex!" "What is sex, Sarah? In actual reality, it is merely an act of rubbing organs.

But it leads to so much pleasure. In fact, this particular activity has the potential to stimulate most of our senses."

"Why do some religious people detest sex? Why do so many gurus and religious leaders advise us to keep away from sex?"

"Probably because they don't know how to handle it in a befitting manner." "Befitting manner? What's that?"

"Would you like to have a treatise on the subject, Madam, or would you like a practical demonstration?"

She blushed and threw a tiny cushion at him out of embarrassment, not knowing how to respond.

But she was not the kind to get distracted easily, hence she quickly regained her poise. "Seriously Arun, tell me, why is there such a hang-up about this simple act of life?"

"Because social, cultural and religious upbringing differs from person to person."

"Animals have no hang-ups about sex. They don't suffer from impotency or frigidity. You don't hear about animals suffering from sexually transmitted diseases in spite of a frequent change of partners."

"Why is there so much suffering associated with sex?"

"Because we have made it 'not easily available'. If it was easily available, there would not be so much hype about it."

"We have messed around with sex for generations. There are people for whom sex is a tool to dissipate excessive congestion in their genitals, for some it is for the survival of their family lineage.

There are some people who love to be sensuously stimulated. There are some who use sex as a power game against their partners.

Alternatively, it can also be used as a means to connect with their partner out of love, to feel reassured emotionally, as a symbol of care and unconditional acceptance.

There are some people who love to express their sexuality and feelings with the process of love making.

There are some who use this tool for stimulation of their creativity. And there are some who use sex to experience oneness with their partner." "What do you use sex for?" "Do you want me to be honest? When I slept with you, the first feeling was of physical relief. There was a lot I had held back for a long time. So, you helped me to release my pent-up physical needs. After a while, I started enjoying the sensuous pleasures, your mere presence around me would provide. At times even seeing you coming out of the bathroom with a towel around your body... in fact every gesture...your smile..., every movement of your body had left a lasting sensuous impression in my heart. I simply loved it."

"Loved it?" Sarah was losing objectivity now.

"No, I still love it and I loved to reciprocate it too in my own special ways, until suddenly one fine day you turned cold in Maldives."

"You were continuously talking about your ex-girlfriend and I could not take it anymore. Certainly not during the moments of intimacy!"

"So, you went into a power game by closing up and physically rejecting me." Sarah smiled but Arun was serious. Sarah felt queer as Arun's words turned into butterflies in her stomach.

I hope he does not pick up a fight on this again.

"I am sorry." "No, I am sorry, I got caught in your power game, I should not have done it. Thank God you put your arms down."

"Power game? You mean to say I was in a power game?"

"Isn't your physical and emotional rejection an attempt to gain one-upmanship?"

"No!" she became defensive.

Arun got up to make a drink for both of them. She was all alone near the swimming pool.

She followed him to the dining room, put her arms around him and kissed him on his back.

"I see your point, Arun, but I am not prepared to believe that I could be in a power game with you. It sounds so horrible to do that to the one you love. Can that not be a natural response of a woman who is in love with a man, who in a drunken state while making love to her, keeps calling out to his ex?"

"All right, Sarah, I agree I did what you say. But so, what?"

"So what? The message is loud and clear to me that I am not the only woman in your life. You are using my body to complete your 'incompletions' with your ex. I don't think any woman with self-respect would allow it."

"A woman with total self-respect would definitely take it. Because she does not depend on others to gain respect. The problem with you is that you haven't been able to develop self-respect, so you allow yourself to be used by others and then you feel used in the name of love. You felt used by me too."

"Yes, I did." She was getting terribly upset. "I never mentioned that, but I felt so cheap about myself."

"So, you thought of disconnecting from me. Disconnecting when I was trying to connect to you? Besides, was I left with any option? What did you get by disconnecting from me?" He turned his back away from her to go to the bedroom. His tone was becoming angrier.

"At least I did not feel cheap about myself," Sarah countered. "Did it not occur to you that your behavior could make me feel cheap about myself? If at the drop of a hat you can feel used, couldn't you consider the possibility of me having some sort of history too? No benefit of the doubt where I am concerned? Can't I have any human weakness?" His eyes were red and he almost had tears in his eyes.

"That's what I thought and that's what brought me back to you. I am sorry." "Sorry?"

Both of them broke into laughter. "Promise me that if you feel hurt you are not going to behave like that ever again. Come and talk to me. Tell me what hurt you. I didn't even know I was talking about my 'ex' in my drunken state. Had you told me, rather than keeping quiet or shrinking away from me, I would have done something about it. We would have immediately talked about it."

"I was scared you would not like it."

"You think I liked your indifference to me any better?"

She said nothing and gave him a kiss. His anger melted. Almost automatically, he put his hands around her waist and pulled her closer.

"I am sorry, I was at fault too," Arun paused to assess her response. "Well, we are still together. I am glad, and that is what counts." She bent over him and kissed the side of his neck.

They had enjoyed physical intimacy so many times before, but this was a different experience for both of them. She almost felt as if, along with the layers of clothes, they were removing layers of barriers between each other.

While exploring his body, Sarah felt she was trying to understand the essence of each precious element of his being. Every cell of his body felt different today. Today she wanted to get so close to him, that even his skin felt like a hindrance.

Arun felt the difference too. He was more demanding with her, as if her entire body belonged to him. He was sucking her all over, each and every finger, her nose, her ears, "Umhh! What are you doing!"

"I want all the goodness that you have today. You feel totally mine, much more than ever before."

He buried his head in between her lovely breasts. I wish I had a key to open up your ribcage and reach out to your heart."

Holding his head in both her arms, she guided his lips to her left nipple. "You can extract all my love from here. It is all for you."

Love making was a different experience for both of them. Arun was in no hurry to enter her. It was not about a temporary high and then falling apart to be in their different worlds. Today, both of them wished that these moments would never end.

"Arun." Sarah woke him up from his trance-like state. "It's been four hours since we went to bed. Aren't you hungry?"

"No, I am feeling quite full." He put his hands on her chest. "Do you feel like eating?"

"I do, but I don't want to waste a second. I want to make the best out of these precious moments that I have with you."

"Thank you so much. I love you. I wouldn't mind some coffee, though." Sarah quickly went to the kitchen and fetched coffee with cookies to eat. "Delicious. You make the best coffee, Sarah. You were telling me that you wanted to do something special, isn't it? I think you should start a coffee shop." "Nope! My coffee is only for you. I don't think I would be able to make coffee this good for anyone else. And of course, someone has to be really in love with me to call this coffee the best coffee in the world," Sarah laughed.

"Oh, if that is the case, forget about the coffee shop. I don't want so many people falling in love with you."

"Arun, do you ever feel possessive about me?"

"Perhaps yes, but I am sure that the feeling will pass one day." "No, I would feel good if you behaved possessively about me." "But I don't feel good because when I feel possessive about you, I feel you don't belong to me. You are not me."

"What!" Sarah exclaimed.

"I am waiting for the day when I feel one with you. I know conceptually it is possible, but I am not feeling that way from within yet."

She felt perplexed by his response.

The level of possessiveness is inversely proportional to the level of security. The more possessive we feel about anything, the more insecure we are about it.

Chapter Six

Both of them chose to conclude the beautiful day with a special dinner in a roof-top restaurant, from where they could get a view of the innumerable bright lights shining in the entire town. It had been a long time since they'd had such a relaxed and yet meaningful day. She looked at the open dark sky in the night and tried looking out for stars and their constellations. She remembered her good old days on the farm, when she used to gaze at them so enthusiastically. Comparatively, the Mumbai sky showed very few stars... Perhaps many of them had descended on the town to enjoy the excitement of the city... and of course two of them had chosen to shine through Arun's eyes too. Just then she realized that those two little stars were intently looking at her and waiting for her to finish her fantasy trip.

She looked into Arun's eyes as if she was still searching for something, while Arun patiently watched Sarah engrossed in her thought process.

It was an unusual silence. The waiter served water and placed the menu card on their table, after deliberating for a while whether he should disturb the lovely couple immersed in each other.

With a sip of water, Sarah brought herself back in touch with the restaurant environment and made an effort to finish the customary formality of consulting each other and requesting their choice of meal. For a change, it did not matter to Sarah what was being ordered for dinner, because she was hungry for something else.

"My question still remains unanswered. What do I do that is meaningful?" "The main question is, what is meaningful to you?" That was Arun, the expert at responding to one question with another.

Bombarding of questions becomes necessary at times to get clarity in the thinking process.

"I really don't know that Arun. Had I known that I would have started working on it long ago," Sarah reasoned helplessly.

"Was finding a guru a meaningful exercise for you?" Though this question seemed harmless, Sarah was taken by surprise and seemed to be shaken out of her chain of thought.

"Are you teasing me, Arun?" Sarah asked.

"No, I am not teasing you. But in the literal sense, I am teasing your thought process."

She kept her gaze on the lamp. The soft music in the background of the roof-top restaurant made the ambience just right to touch upon this very sensitive topic.

"Arun, the human mind is funny. I know I really don't need a Guru, but I am still searching for one."

"Sarah, the irony is, we seldom look out for our exact needs."

"Then what do we look out for?" Sarah was a bit quizzical but patient with his approach.

"We look out for the means and not the goal. It is perfectly fine to do so, but if we get attached to the means, we lose our focus on the goal."

"I did not follow."

A loaded statement takes its own time to sink into the depths of our minds.

"You were, or rather, you are looking out for a guru. Am I right?" She nodded.

"Tell me, why?"

"Because I believe that there is something I need to know which only a guru can tell me."

Sarah knew she was sounding silly, but she had always been honest and transparent with Arun.

"But what is it exactly? Have you tried looking at it?" Arun pursued in his special style of self-discovery.

"I don't know exactly, but some information, some enlightenment, probably a key to the higher purpose in life or something of that sort...."

"Let's talk about the higher purpose in life, because I have heard these words from you several times." Arun leaned forward and adjusted the food plates while the waiter served them lentil soup and masala papad.

"Higher purpose is something which is extraordinary, far above human existence, something great! You know, Arun, I don't have the words to explain what I am looking for," Sarah mentioned in a resigned tone.

"Do you at least have a concept or vision?" Arun realized that the soup was getting cold but he chose to focus on his conversation with Sarah.

"Are you upset with me?" Sarah asked, expecting Arun to get impatient with her confused state of mind.

"No," Arun displayed a lot of patience. With his hand, Arun gently drew her attention back to her soup, hoping that sipping on it would give her some time to mull over her thoughts.

Sarah took his unspoken advice seriously.

Just as she began to speak, she felt something choke in her throat. She had swallowed more of the soothing warm liquid, hoping to clear the passage, as she prepared to confess to Arun.

We feel choked when our throat muscles go into a spasm. These muscles respond to the feeling of not being OK. We don't feel okay about ourselves when we feel guilty, or ashamed of having done something which our preconditioning forbids.

Sarah cleared her throat, "I am feeling guilty at a certain level. Actually, before coming to India, I had so many questions which I wanted to be answered by a guru, but I have found my answers to almost all those questions during my conversations with you."

Arun placed his soup spoon on the side plate. He leaned slightly with his fingers interlocked behind his head and silently listened to Sarah, knowing fully well that he had succeeded in his mission for the day.

"You have diluted my immense craving for a guru to a great extent, but there is still a part of me which is looking out for a guru."

Arun smiled as he waited for her to continue.

"I am feeling incomplete without a guru. I've put too many things at stake to find one."

Sarah took a deep breath as if she needed to get some fresh air to break this stalemate.

"You are likely to put too many things at stake in the future too," Arun's tone was slightly sarcastic as he blurted out these strong words.

"I was scared of telling you that I still have this yearning."
"Why? Sarah, why were you scared?" Arun asked as if he knew the answer but still wanted it to come from the horse's mouth.

The main course was ready to be served, so Sarah took that time to ponder over this question.

Sarah took a bite of the 'naan' and focused on the stuffed green bell pepper on her plate. She was not hungry, but the food was a good excuse to buy some time in order to carefully collect her thoughts. Sarah managed to gulp down the food through her constricted gullet with the help of a glass of water. Then she began to put together the words, to convey her thoughts with sensitivity, yet with firmness.

"Arun, somewhere I know you don't believe in 'gurus'. I also know that you have given me much more than my expectations of a guru. I realize you make me understand myself much more than a guru ever would. After meeting so many of those so-called gurus, my faith in finding one is diminishing." On hearing her own words, the dull expression on her face vanished and her eyes twinkled with the new insight that had just dawned upon her. She took several minutes to reflect on what she said. "Yes, that is the thing. I am losing faith in myself."

"Not a guru?" Arun asked.

"Perhaps I am losing faith in the possibility of finding an ideal guru." Sarah's energy appeared to have dropped a bit, which became evident as she slouched on the sofa, as if she was suddenly very tired.

"I still don't understand. Why do you need a Guru?" Sarah felt discouraged with Arun's questioning on the need for a guru.

Pretending to have completed his dinner, Arun got up from his seat and joined Sarah on her sofa. He realized that this discussion was taking a reverse turn, when Sarah came up with a question.

"Arun, why are you so against the concept of a guru?" What was a sensitive topic for Sarah was becoming a touchy one for him too. "No, Sarah, I am not against gurus. They are doing a great job.

I am against those who, under the garb of being a guru; take advantage of their disciples' weaknesses. I am against those who greedily chase gurus or those who helplessly become dependent on them. None of them serve the purpose. 'Guru Pratha' was a beautiful Indian tradition. A guru was a major milestone in everyone's life and not the final destination. A genuine guru attempted to guide his disciples to the path which took them to self-empowerment, and not a path which ended towards himself."

A guru was needed to keep the ego and ignorance in check, but some of the disciples have made 'guru' an issue of ego out of sheer ignorance.

"Sarah, after the trauma that I experienced in my previous relationship, I felt a need to know why. I kept asking myself this question, 'Why me'?" He took a pause to reflect.

"Like you, I firmly believed that only a guru could answer my question. I tried searching for one the way you did after coming to India, but I got disillusioned by most."

Arun took some time to reflect.

"But that's my experience," he added, quickly recovering from his journey back in time.

It's pointless generalizing individual experiences and perceptions.

"I am sure there are genuine gurus."

Finding a guru was his paramount desire which made him grow in life.

That perhaps was the reason why he could have so much empathy for Sarah.

Thanks to his disillusionment, he began to look within for answers and gradually started getting them.

Had he not read so many books, met so many gurus, spent hours together meditating and mastering breath work, going into prolonged self-introspection at the farmhouse, he would have turned into a shattered personality after the agonizing pain of rejection.

"Sarah, I have done it all."

Sarah was slightly scared of witnessing Arun's emotional vulnerability.

She gently suggested, "Let us go home." "Would you care for some dessert?" Arun offered.

"No, my life is overflowing with your sweetness and that is more than enough." These words were not from her usual glossary.

Arun looked into her eyes to assess the solidarity behind her statement to see if she was joking or being serious.

Our eyes invariably project the truth. If you want to understand a person, look deep into their eyes.

"I love you, Sarah. I love you just the way you are."

She affectionately leaned her head on his shoulder and waited for the attendant to process the credit card.

It appeared to be a long drive back home. Every minute felt extended. Intuitively, she knew that something important was going to happen that day.

Back home, Arun led her to the swimming pool area and ushered her to sit next to him on his recliner. Arun had ordered this lovely broad recliner, large enough to accommodate both of them. It had a velvet lining and was ergonomically designed with the right amount of firmness to facilitate total relaxation.

Both of them lay there looking at the vast expanse of an awesome clear sky.

In the city of Mumbai, it is difficult to find the sky clear. *This appears to be a special night,* Sarah thought. "There is magic in the air. Something special is going to happen," she thought aloud.

"How do you know?" Arun's attention was back to her again after a short span of drifting into his past.

"I just know it," she continued, looking at the sky.

"Does that happen to you all the time, Sarah?"

"No, that happens often but most of the time I don't want to know it. So, I ignore it." Then suddenly she propped herself up to face Arun with a question, "Am I wrong in feeling this way, Arun?"

"No, Sarah, it is okay to feel that way." Sarah felt relaxed as she felt okay about herself. Though Sarah constantly needed Arun's approval, she was quite aware that Arun always disapproved of her need for approval.

"Arun, what is intuition? I know that I know. I mean, I would find the answer to this question within myself but I want to understand it from you."

"You answered your question. ***Intuition is knowing that you know.***" "But I don't trust myself that I know," Sarah clasped both her hands in exasperation.

"Sarah, we all know what we are supposed to be knowing. ***We need to trust our knowingness. The key to all the knowledge***

that we ever need, lies in our subconscious mind. We need to just zone into it."

"Why don't we do it?" She turned her face towards Arun.

"I will explain that to you. But, before that, will you tell me your exact age?"

"28 years, three months and five days. She felt thrilled at her quick calculation.

"Sarah, what was my question?" "What's my exact age?"

"No, think again."

"Arun, you asked me my exact age."

"No, my question was, 'WILL YOU' tell me your exact age?"

"Yes, I will," she giggled. She knew she had goofed up. The logical answer to his question was 'yes' or 'no'.

"I got it. I admit I messed up." She impulsively stuck out her tongue. She looked like a little baby with this funny gesture.

"Sarah, it is not you, but your conditioned mind which goofed up. It is your conditioning which does not allow any information to go in or come out without distortion."

"I understand what you are trying to say."

"Sarah, I firmly believe that our mind already has all the answers that we will ever need. We need to learn the art of finding them out."

"How does one cultivate this art?"

"By learning how to keep your mind still."

A still mind is like still water. The more disturbed the water, the more difficult it is to see through and the same is true for the mind.

"At any point of time, we have so many relevant or irrelevant thought processes going on, that the information that we seek gets distorted or diluted. When our mind is disturbed with preconditioning and disturbing thought processes and the resultant emotions, we find it difficult to absorb or extract any relevant information in an untainted manner." He sounded like a seasoned professor of philosophy.

Sarah was completely absorbed in what he had to say.

"That's why we should take maximum advantage of our mind when we are about to fall asleep or just when we wake up. At this time, the mind goes into a state, where we can easily access and process relevant information."

"Is that something called Alfa state you are talking about?"

"Sarah, I am talking about common sense. Whenever we have lesser thoughts, either with meditation or with some other techniques, we are more intuitive because the mind is still."

"Umhh!" that was Sarah's way of saying she was listening with rapt attention.

"So, learn to be in a meditative space and ask questions. Initially you may feel the stars are answering your questions or your angel guides are answering you."

"How do I know whether the information that I get is pertinent?" Sarah interrupted a bit impatiently.

"You will feel a strange sense of peace and harmony within, when you receive the information from your inner space. It will be just right for you." Arun experienced deep harmony and peace as he spoke these words.

"Arun, what are angel guides? Do you believe in them? Some of the books say that we are each born with two angel guides who are always with us."

"I have spent too many days trying to get in touch with them and now I realized that it doesn't matter who answers my queries so far as I feel one with the universe at the time of listening to the answers."

Arun paused for a while so that Sarah could assimilate the information. "Arun, as a child I used to talk to the stars. I used to see fairies and angels in my room...."

"Then?" Arun enquired.

"My mother thought I was going insane. She started ensuring that I was not left alone at any point of time."

"And?"

"And then I lost the habit. Now as an adult I can't do it." "How old were you at that time Sarah?" "I must have been around four years old."

"Wake up that four-year-old Sarah in you. She knows how to talk to the stars."

There was magic in the air that night. Sarah forgot her age and became a four year-old kid and opened her arms as if she was about to embrace the sky. There was joy on her face, a blissful feeling.

Arun decided not to disturb her and left her to her thoughts for a while. Though her lips were not moving, Arun knew she was talking to the stars and angels.

"Arun," she snapped out of her thoughts suddenly. "Are you sure if I continue like this I won't go insane?"

"Can anybody go insane by talking to oneself? The stars that you are seeing, the angels that you are seeing, are an extension of your own self."

"You mean to say everything is an illusion?"

"Yes, of course, everything is an illusion eventually. So go ahead and talk to the stars."

"What? I mean, I find it difficult to believe that I am hearing this from you."

"Do what I tell you, Sarah," he said with a lot of love. "What do I talk about?" "What would you talk about, if you met an interesting stranger?"

"First of all, I would wonder whether I am worthy of talking to this stranger?"

"Exactly! That is what happens to most people. They think they are not worthy."

People's belief in their worthlessness, distances them from the highest and the best.

He paused knowing well that what he just said applied somewhere to Sarah too.

"Do you want to know, Sarah, why I don't like gurus? Not all, but many of the gurus behave like agents who help you negotiate with someone who is part of you."

She was shocked to hear his description of a guru, waiting for him to say something more.

"Tell me Sarah, who is God?" "I don't know, I haven't met God, but I suppose someone who is supremely powerful and all capable." "How do you know? Have you experienced it personally?" "No, but I presume so after reading some of the literature and scriptures."

With great alarm she turned towards him, "Don't tell me you don't believe in God!"

"I don't have to believe in God, Sarah, because I am God."

"Wwwwhh.... What?"

"Yes! Tell me," taking her baby finger in his hand, "is this your finger?" "Yes, it is very much a part of me."

"Sarah, if I get a cell of this baby finger, is it theoretically possible to separate the DNA and clone it to make a brand-new Sarah?"

"Yes, theoretically it is possible." "Why?"

"Because I have the same genetic coding in all my cells." "Because?" Arun pursued with his style of self-interrogation. "Because this cell is a part of me."

"Exactly, the way this small micro-cell is a part of you, don't you think you are like a small unit who is part of this entire cosmos?"

"No doubt about it," Sarah nodded her head in agreement. "What is cosmos? Can I call this cosmos God?" Arun asked.

"No, the ruler of the cosmos is God," Sarah was slightly defensive as her core belief was getting attacked.

"Who is the ruler of your body?" Arun persevered. "My soul."

"Sarah, the soul needs you as much as your body needs this soul. You are inseparable till the time you die. We are connected to this entire cosmos in the same way as the cells of your body are connected to each other through a common vital force, which you may call the soul. You are in each and every cell right?"

Sarah nodded her head in agreement.

"Now, compare the cosmos with your body and your existence with that of your cells. As you are in each and every cell of yours, similarly, you represent the cosmos. That means you are the cosmos and you are God, if you think the whole governing force behind this cosmos, is God!!!"

"The cosmos can replace this form of you. Like these cells, the human form is replaceable. But when you are an integral part of the cosmos, however small, you are the cosmos."

"Do you feel the cosmos and God are the same?" Sarah's voice was muffled with confusion.

"What is God, Sarah? It is collective consciousness. Just as you would get affected by pain in any cell of your body, similarly when we go through pain, the 'cosmos' or 'God' will definitely get affected."

"That's why you must know that you are part of the universe. And if you are part of the universe, you are the universe."

If you are the creation and manifestation of God, you have the energy of God flowing within. With the same logic you are God.

"For years, society and the agents of most religions have made us feel so low about ourselves, putting God on a very high, unattainable pedestal. These so-called representatives of God have done a lot of harm by perpetuating the fear of God and thus controlling lesser mortals.

God, and God consciousness cannot be experienced by those who are afraid, or by those who feel low about themselves. To experience God, one has to feel one with God, with God's creations.

God consciousness is a Supreme Intelligence, which is very sensitively and sensibly governing this entire universe. The purpose is to grow in our own consciousness by remaining in touch with our own God consciousness. There is always wonderful guidance available to all of us. And some of us who open up to it can easily access it."

"Yes, I gather from what you have told me that ***the universal intelligence is a pool of all information. If we learn to zone in correctly, we can gather any information to expand our limited human understanding***," Sarah tried summarizing in some simple words.

"Was that the mechanism through which you could know what was happening to me?" Sarah had always been intrigued by his capacity to correctly guess what was going on with her. Was this the key?

"This is the way I try to get information as and when I need it."

"Oh, how wonderful! Who did you learn it from? Can you teach me too?" Sarah was full of excitement.

"No, it happened at the time when I was left all alone. I had no one to answer my queries, so I started throwing the questions open to the universe, hoping that someone up there would listen to me and reciprocate."

Sarah kept listening to him spellbound.

"Initially I would get my answers through my dreams, later I would just stumble upon a headline in a newspaper which would make some sense to me.

Sometimes I would go to a library or a bookstore and something would compel me to pick up a particular book. Usually, the first line on the first page that opened felt like the exact / most appropriate answer or clue to my questions."

As Arun appeared to be lost in his past experiences, Sarah took some time out to reflect upon her experiences where she had spontaneously got answers like this. But those never satisfied her. Probably she wanted those answers from a guru in a human form.

"When my mother died, I was left all alone. Dipti was studying abroad. There were a few relatives and Ramu Chacha. I did not feel belonged. I started feeling very lonely and I would talk to imaginary figures in the room. Later I was told that they were my angel guides."

"How wonderful! So, you grew up talking to angels and fairies? I wish my mother had allowed me to do that."

"I could not see them well so I did not know who they were but they were definitely helpful."

"I would ask a question and they would answer me. They would put me to sleep. They would help me with my studies. They have done a lot for me, Sarah."

"One of the reasons why I can do without many friends around me all the time is because they are always there to give me company. I always feel their presence."

Sarah was astonished. He had not shared this secret with her before. "I talk to them even when I am driving. But, now-a-days, I don't talk to them as much."

"Why?" Sarah asked naively.

"Because they have gifted me a beautiful fairy. These days whenever I feel lonely, I talk to this fairy."

Sarah felt so excited. "Can I see this fairy too?"

"Of course!" Arun leaned closer to her face and looked into her eyes. Sarah began to feel foolish about her question.

"Look into my eyes and you will see this living fairy called Sarah."

Sarah felt silly but yet she loved this romantic gesture. She melted in his arms. She spent the rest of the night looking at the stars and cherishing the wonderful intimacy she was experiencing with Arun.

It is human conditioning which keeps us away from bliss. The more we become deconditioned, the more bliss we experience.

She started spending more and more time by herself. She would lie on the recliner, trying to connect to the universe.

She would ask questions and patiently wait for the answers.

Initially, she wouldn't get the answers directly but she started getting lots of dreams.

"Dreams are expressions of the subconscious mind. What you see in the form of a dream is something that your subconscious mind wants to eliminate or inform you about."

She started interpreting her dreams in her own special way.

"Arun, I feel horrible that I can't talk to my angel guides and masters the way you talk to yours," Sarah complained one evening, over a cup of coffee, leaning against the terrace parapet, watching the sun setting into the ocean.

"You haven't yet. Replace your CANNOT with NOT YET.

When you say you can't, for sure you will not be able to. But if you say you haven't yet, you remain open to a future possibility.

"Besides, your feeling of non-communication with them is your perception. ***Always check your silent conversation. Every thought of yours is a powerful energy...."***

The good student in Sarah got busy, checking her own internal conversation.

"You might be interacting in your own special way. Each one of us is unique. You don't have to wait to listen to them. You can listen to your own self."

"How?"

"When you go to sleep at night, think of a question and watch for the answer in the form of a dream or direct conversation or some meaningful incident in your life. You will know when you

get a true answer by the kind of peculiar, indescribable blissful sensation."

"I will try and check it out later," said Sarah entering the kitchen. Sarah got busy making green Thai curry for their evening meal.

Arun followed her and watched her movements and the ease with which she moved while working in the kitchen.

"Sarah, how many grams of salt did you put in that curry?" asked Arun as he watched her adding spices in the curry.

"I don't know. Arun I generally reach into the jar and pick up the exact amount of the ingredient needed for cooking that dish."

Sarah got what Arun was trying to convey. She switched off the burner and turned to him, "Who makes me do that?" Arun chose not to answer her question and just kept quiet. He waited for Sarah to finish with her own thought process and then chose to give her some more food for thought.

"You think that the great pieces of art that artists create, the great music that musicians play, the delicious food that you so often cook, are well- calculated by their creators? No. Great creations are a matter of inspiration, some inner calling, as they say. They are all zoning in to the universal guidance."

"The curry that you are preparing is ready in some other reality, and you are simply manifesting it in this reality."

"Sounds interesting," Sarah threw her shoulders slightly forward and upward in an attempt to show her agreement.

"We all know what we need to do. It is our logical mind, our conditioning and our emotions which keep us away from this knowingness."

"That's true. This magic cooking touch does not work well when I am angry. I tend to forget what to do when I am sad or upset. I do it best when I am in sync with my flow."

"I am talking about that flow Sarah, learn to identify the moments when you are in this flow. You could be in the flow when you are bathing, when you are singing, when you are dancing. Gradually, ***as you master the art of remaining in synchronicity with the flow, you will always do the right thing at the right time.***"

"Is that what being in meditation is all about?"

"Sarah, ***meditation is a way of life. The rest are techniques leading to that state - the state of being in the flow of universal intelligence.***"

"Did you consult anyone before you married me?" "No, because I knew it was right for me at that moment."

"Exactly! We have a knowingness about everything in life. So, coming to your question, what should you be doing in life? Sarah, ask this question to no one but yourself." "Only you are capable of answering this question."

"What if the answer that I get is not the right one?" Sarah's forehead wrinkled as she expressed her doubt.

"What if the choice you made about marrying me was not the right one?"

"Then I would have passed it off as an experience and moved on with my life."

"That is exactly what I am telling you. What could go wrong? What could be the worst scenario, if you follow your own inner voice?"

"Nothing really. But where is my inner voice?"

"Inside you. Give yourself some time and be still. It will be audible."

For many days, after that, Sarah would sit with her legs crossed and wait for the inner voice to tell her something. But nothing happened and it was becoming more and more frustrating with each passing day and she was left with no choice but to complain to Arun.

"What is it that you do when you sit alone, Sarah? I mean, how do you meditate?"

"Isn't it like this?" Sarah showed her cross-legged and upright position with thumb and index finger touching in the perfect 'Chin Mudra'. I close my eyes and allow no thought to come. But keeping away thoughts during the meditation is very tough."

Arun looked at her with a lot of compassion. "Today, ***when you meditate, don't worry about your thoughts. You meditate on your thoughts.***"

Now that's new. How does one do that? thought Sarah.

"Meditate on my thoughts? No guru has ever taught me to do that.

Anyway, since you are telling me, I will try doing it."

"You don't have to do it because I am telling you, darling. It is logical. Our thoughts are our reality. Not having thoughts, itself is a thought. So, in fact if you want to focus, focus on your thoughts. Observe your thoughts and see where they are leading you and watch for the sensations these thoughts create in your body."

"What if I get some crappy thoughts, Arun?"

"Now what's that?" Arun knew what she meant, but it was important for him to question her so that she got clarity.

"Say for example the thought of sex, or money or my past miseries." "That's very good. These are the areas which are seeking your attention, so, pay attention to them before you move forward.

Even after you remove the boiling liquid away from the fire, it is natural that the bubbles will come up, releasing the trapped gases and vapor. After a while the process will subside and the liquid will stabilize."

"The mind is like that liquid, the fire is constant feedback from the world around you, which keeps stimulating your senses and thought process. If you take the mind away from these stimuli, you will get some bubbling for a while but they will have no choice but to subside."

"We unnecessarily try trapping the undesirable thoughts and feelings inside because we feel ashamed of the process of letting go."

Sarah took Arun's advice seriously and unleashed her thought process.

As she tried meditating on the first day, a lot of anger surfaced. She did not understand the anger, hence she called up Arun.

"Arun, I am feeling so much anger inside me. I don't even know what to do with this anger. I don't even know exactly why I'm feeling this anger!"

Arun said, "rub your knees and say aloud: 'Even though I am holding on to this anger, I heal and integrate that part of me…'."

She followed his instructions to the T.

"Now repeat this sentence two more times while rubbing your knees." Obediently, Sarah did exactly that.

"Now put both your hands on the center of your chest and take seven deep breaths. If you still experience the anger, repeat the entire process, once again."

She did as Arun had instructed. It worked. The anger subsided. But sadness surfaced.

This time she repeated the entire process, keeping the sadness in her mind.

While rubbing her knees, she affirmed thrice, "Even though I am feeling sad and sorry for myself, still I heal and integrate that part of me." After affirming, she put both her hands on her chest and gently rubbed the center. She felt so relieved and calm. Until the evening she was busy acknowledging each feeling and emotion surfacing in her mind and in a short while, she felt so quiet and calm. Thinking was almost an effort now.

Sarah started feeling relaxed, and a little drowsy. She went to lie on her bed for a little while.

In this half-awake state, with her eyes slightly open, a vision appeared in her mind's eye. She saw a beautiful retreat center with a central meditation hall. There were beautiful pyramid-like structures all around. She saw therapy rooms, she saw the movement of people, she saw some people doing yoga, some receiving therapy or massages, some reading books in a library. It appeared to be an awesome environment. Her eyes flew open.

What is this being shown to me?

The voice from within said, "A healing retreat center." She jerked out of that state. She could not believe what she had just heard and seen.

She was zapped. She lay on her bed with her eyeballs fixed on the movement of the ceiling fan above her bed. She turned her eyes to the right and saw Arun standing and watching her. He had not even removed his necktie, so he had probably just entered the room.

"You heard the voice?" he suspected.

"Yes.... But how do I know that is what it is? How do I know it was not my imagination?"

"If you simply had to imagine it, why did you struggle so much? Remember, Sarah, ***there is no such thing like imagination. Even these great artists who imagine, somehow zone into something that is existing in some other realm."***

"I don't believe this."

"All right, ask your mind to give you some proof in seven days." She did exactly that.

On the evening of the third day after the incident, the doorbell rang, and she saw Dipti standing at the door.

"May I come in?"

"Of course. This is your house too."

"No, Sarah, this belongs to you and Arun. Thanks for allowing me inside," she continued her conversation as she settled down on a sofa.

"After the drama that I created before your wedding, I don't think I deserve to be treated so well by you."

"C'mon, Dipti that happened in the past. We are completely over it. Arun still loves you very much."

"And you?"

"Honestly, I am neutral. To a great extent, I am grateful to you. You made me realize how much I loved Arun."

Sarah settled down comfortably in front of her.

"I felt so lonely after the two of you left the farmhouse. I felt horrible inside. The same people are taking care of the house but I see so many challenges coming my way. The plants are dying one by one, pests are troubling us. Whenever I look at the farm, I feel deep regret."

Sarah looked at her to find out how genuine she was.

"You know, I thought that Arun loved the farm more than anything or anyone. That's why I asked him to choose between the farm and you. He chose you over me and the farm. I was so jealous. I didn't want to see your face."

Sarah wanted to change the topic. She even interrupted with an offer of drinks.

“Let me complete, Sarah. Tomorrow I am flying back to L.A. Before that, I want to take the load off my chest.”

“Can I offer you some coffee?” Sarah really felt quite awkward. She wished Arun had been present.

“Yes please. You make the best coffee in the world. That’s what my dear brother always said.” The compliment appeared genuine, still Sarah was not so sure of Dipti’s intentions.

“Dipti, ***when a person is in love, he loses rationality***,” Sarah tried to show her modesty.

“If this is being irrational, I am glad that he is irrational,” Dipti made the statement of the year. But it was too late, today this stuff did not make any difference to Sarah.

“I don’t think anybody can make him as happy as you have made him,” Dipti continued.

“You are flattering me, Dipti.” Sarah was getting slightly embarrassed.

The doorbell rang and Sarah sighed out of relief. She knew it was Arun from the mere sound of it.

“Hey, Dipti!”

He threw his bag on the sofa to give her a big hug. He almost lifted her and raised her up like a small child in his arms.

“What a great surprise! How are you? When did you come?” he gushed.

"Oh, I am so sorry, I am not even giving you time to say anything." Gently he lowered her onto the sofa. He sat very close to her, almost leaning.

Sarah watched the show peeping from the kitchen. She had tears of joy in her eyes. For a change she did not feel uneasy about her presence and the close interaction between the two of them. She did not even feel threatened by her.

Instead, she prepared coffee for both of them and settled down on the sofa opposite them.

"I keep getting the news about both of you from Ramu Chacha. You nut case! You should have tried to contact me some time."

"Dipti, I missed you so much. But I wanted you to have some time to heal the wounds that have been caused by my decision."

"Yes, I thought and waited, that if not me, you would at least miss the farmhouse and come to visit sometime, but you did not."

"I missed both. But I can do without the farmhouse. I am glad that you are looking after it."

"No, Arun, the plants are dying without the two of you." Dipti pleaded.

"Please take charge of the farm and farmhouse. I don't think it is my cup of tea. This is the only ancestral property that we both have inherited. I realize it is not about my right, but about the nurturance of the property."

"Dipti, it is too late. I am doing well as an IT consultant here. I have taken up quite a few projects. I have hired so many software engineers for the job. I can't leave all of this and return to the farm."

He took a pause to sip the coffee.

"Gone are the days when I used to get assignments and fulfil them sitting there at the farmhouse. Now I have an entire team who seek guidance from me on a daily basis."

"Let Sarah handle it," Dipti blurted out.

"What do I do all alone in the house if Sarah is not with me?" Dipti bit her tongue.

"My heart hurts. I am going back to L.A. Peter wants me back in his life. These are the property papers. I am surrendering to you the entire property legally and officially, forever.

"Dipti, you always make decisions in haste and want others to follow them. Do you realize that you have put us in a jam now? There is no way we could actively do farming," Arun was disappointed. "Then open some sort of retreat center!" Sarah's jaw dropped.

"You can have yoga and meditation facilities at the retreat center. You guys can go and supervise it once in a while."

I have already talked to Peter about the plan a month ago. He is even ready to fund it and help you with marketing for overseas customers.

"You had decided about it a month ago, Dipti?" Arun appeared a bit upset. "It was all in the planning stage. I realize that I can't plan for you. But I would sincerely request you to take it over." She handed over the bunch of papers requesting Sarah to take it.

Sarah was stunned. *Life cannot take this strange a turn!* She was trying hard to balance herself, hence did not extend her palms and remained seated. Dipti almost dumped the bunch in her lap and got up to leave the house.

"Won't you give me a parting hug, bro?"

He got up and gave her a tight, warm hug. "I knew it and so did you, Dipti, that the farmhouse is something that would have not fascinated you for a long time. Why did you snatch it away from me then?"

"I expected you to beg me for it. And I thought I would be able to barter it and get Sarah out of your life."

She took a deep breath as her eyes brimmed with tears. "But I was wrong."

"Please forgive me Arun, for being so hard on you. ***Now I understand the difference between love and possessiveness.***"

She hugged him and left the house.

"I can't believe this!" Sarah was still stunned and could not get up from the sofa. "I had asked for simple proof!"

Before Sarah could recover, Arun had already moved ahead to the next level, "Sarah, there are many visionaries who have lots and lots of plans. But ***successful people are those who get their plans and visions implemented.***"

Chapter Seven

Nothing can be more relaxing than watching a vast ocean in action, especially when you are in the middle of it, with no sight of land anywhere. Sarah chose to accompany Arun to Goa for an important business conference. For the return journey to Mumbai, he decided to separate from the group to spend some time with his sweetheart; and to Sarah's greatest thrill, he chose to take a cruise.

Standing on the upper deck, leaning against the iron railings, watching the sea waves, Sarah could not help but compare the sea with life.

She had been puzzled about some recent events and especially the surprise Dipti had given them. Probably this was the right time to think about it. "Arun, explain to me what made Dipti change so much?"

"You see, Sarah, we all are here for a definite core learning," the philosopher in Arun emerged to satisfy the seeker soul in Sarah.

"Agreed. But how does one know what that lesson is?"

Short cuts take away much needed interesting learning and experiences, yet invariably we tend to look for the fastest and easiest way out.

"We are here to learn how to respond in creative and constructive ways to the challenges of life. The universe keeps throwing in opportunities for you, hoping you may respond in different ways. But most of us respond in the same fashion as we have always done in the past. Those who manage to remain wise observers, break out of these loops and move forward in life." He realized that he talked like a preacher. Sarah listened to him almost speechless, going back in her own life to examine her life's circumstances.

"We need to learn to respond in a creative and constructive manner to similar kinds of challenges in life."

He thought it prudent to sum up what he had said for further clarity. This was a loaded sentence and Sarah found it somewhat strenuous to handle. She was not prepared for this kind of heavy discussion on this lovely, leisurely and romantic short break in the middle of the sea.

Sarah walked towards the sea-facing bench and remained glued there for a long time, as her mind travelled down memory lane to check the kind of pattern of circumstances she had been inviting in her life.... Almost all individuals, especially the men whom she had attracted so far, had made her feel low about herself. Most of them made her feel used. *Did they use me or did I allow myself to be used, in the hope of getting something else?* Her tears welled up as she thought of her past.

Arun patiently waited for her to continue the conversation. He knew that a tender chord had been struck.

"Arun, I can see a pattern in my life. Almost all major circumstances have made me feel worthless eventually...the way my mom left me... the way others used me... the way my father eventually rejected me... the way Dipti treated me...my inability to find a guru for myself...even your care and love at times made me feel worthless."

"That's it. Even being happily married and living comfortably in our beautiful apartment has made you feel worthless. Without breaking this pattern, without understanding your life's learning, had you gone ahead with a new venture, I bet you would have felt worthless once again."

"Now I understand why you dissuaded me in a subtle manner."

Arun smiled with a lot of love as he sat down while kneeling on the wooden floor, facing Sarah with his reassuring hands on her knees.

"What could have been an opposite and empowering experience?" "Feeling of being worthy? But how can I feel worthy when I feel that I am not. Won't I be cheating myself, Arun?"

"Sarah, the feeling of worthlessness was a response you chose... all those circumstances where you chose to feel worthless, you could have chosen conversely. You could have chosen to feel worthy too."

Sarah felt like a dumb and illiterate student in a Ph.D. class.

"Let's take an example. Your mom left you and you felt worthless. You could have responded to the same situation in a more empowering manner by realizing that your mom thought you were mature enough to handle your affairs and your dad too."

"Exactly. That's what she thought and she tried explaining that to me."

Both of them remained silent for a long time. She needed the silence. Arun needed it too.

As he was counselling Sarah, a part of him reminded him that he needed the same counsel himself.

“Dipti too had come here to experience contentment, but she chose to play the drama of the deprived one. She felt deprived when I was born and our parents’ attention got divided. She felt deprived when they left us all alone to fend for ourselves. She felt deprived when relatives took advantage and stripped us off a major chunk of the property. She felt deprived without a boyfriend, she felt deprived of genuine love, even when she had a boyfriend. When she was in India, she felt deprived of a foreign education. When she went abroad to study, she felt deprived of the comfort of home. When she came here to catch up with me, she felt deprived of my attention towards her.”

“In fact, the more deprived she felt, the more insecure and possessive she became. The more she tried to grab, the more she had to let go. And every time she had to let go, something about her belief of being deprived got further reinforced.”

“She knew about her basic life script but did not want to get out of it. Feeling deprived and fighting for her so-called human rights had become her passion and comfort zone. I refused to participate when she tried enrolling me in her game. I gave her what she asked for and asked her not to demand anything more than that.”

“She had nothing to complain about, but then she started feeling deprived of my relationship with her. She also felt deprived in the dynamics between her boyfriend and her.”

"So now she has chosen to move out and be with him so that at least she has him in her life."

Arun was getting tired. He changed his position and sat next to her on the wooden bench.

"Why did she surrender the property to you?"

"No, Sarah, it was not surrender. It was a silent deal. A bargain." Sarah was shocked to hear this. "A bargain?" "An exchange. For a relationship with me."

"Aren't you biased, Arun? She might have genuinely surrendered the papers to you," Sarah tried explaining to him.

"Maybe. But that's unlike the Dipti that I have known," Arun was getting uncomfortable with this confrontation from Sarah.

What appears to be hazy due to sheer proximity may appear crystal clear to a distant observer.

"Arun, is the Dipti in your world or the Dipti in my world that cannot do it?"

This was a new confusing twist in the tale. For Sarah to challenge his belief, was a change, which indicated an enhanced sense of self- worth in Sarah. "What do you mean?" Arun tried to hide his irritation.

"Let's see. Is your name Arun?" Though this sounded like a very silly question, Arun intuitively knew something very important and relevant was going to be revealed.

"Yes, so?"

"Is the Arun in my world the same as the Arun in your secretary's world?" Sarah did not wait for him to answer. She was not looking for an answer from him at this point. She was simply asking something that he should have asked himself long back.

"Is the Arun in your secretary's world the same as the Arun in the world of your business partner?"

"You are right, Sarah. I am a different personality for different individuals."

"The Arun in your world is very different compared to the Arun in my business partner's life and in my secretary's life and even in my sister's life."

"So, which is the genuine, original and real Arun?"

"All. What others see is only a part of me."

"No, it is part of them."

"Sorry, I did not understand Sarah."

"Dipti felt deprived, but did you intend to deprive her by any chance?"

"No." Sarah continued. "But still she saw you as the one who deprived her. You tried hard not to get into her game but still she managed to feel deprived by you at some point in time. Knowingly or unknowingly, you played that role because she wanted to see you that way to conform to her belief that the world deprives her."

"Yes, you are right."

"So, your world is the reflection of who you are!"

"You chose to play the lonely one. I got enrolled in your game and it was so easy for me to play indifferent to you until the time I understood your game and chose not to participate in your drama."

"It is not that, Sarah. I identified my own drama and chose not to play that with you. If I had chosen to continue playing the drama of being the lonely one; you would have perhaps continued with your drama of being indifferent, just to continue participating in my drama."

"And I would have continued playing the poor me and the worthless one."

After this 'Aha' moment, they felt amused by their own craziness. They both burst out laughing. They laughed uncontrollably almost to the point of rolling on the floor.

"You know, Sarah, I have seen people repeating the same patterns in their lives again and again. They are aware of their patterns but rarely manage to get out of them."

"They need to have more interesting dramas compared to the one they are playing out at the moment." Sarah said in an all-knowing manner.

"I did not get it, Sarah."

"Look, my 'poor me' act helped me in emotionally blackmailing my parents, making them feel guilty, and finally I could get away being absolutely irresponsible. This went on until you made me realize, that there are benefits as well as penalties for playing such stupid dramas. The penalties were very high."

"Hmm."

"Yes, I was not moving anywhere in life. No wonder I did not get what I wanted in life, because I had to continuously prove the 'worthless poor me' status. My father's disowning me and getting married, and my mother's indifference to me helped me continue playing my drama.

"How did you get out of it, Sarah?"

"Of course with your help. But thanks to Dipti's arrival in my life, finally I was able to leave it behind. You know that."

She could have continued explaining further but an all-knowing smile on Arun's face took away her desire to continue verbal communication.

Sarah got up from the chair to take a stroll on the deck and Arun joined her enjoying the fresh seabreeze. On a sudden impulse, both of them stopped and hugged each other tightly.

"I choose to play the drama of being complete."

Arun tightened his grip on her as if he wanted her to completely get integrated into his being.

They could see a patch of land in the distance. It was the magnificent Mumbai shoreline coming into view. But neither was interested.

If possible, they would have loved to make this cruise a never-ending one. They could have strolled on the deck forever, holding each other in their arms.

"Do you know, Sarah, at a certain level I did the same thing with myself? I played the drama of being unloved. That helped me justify my closing up. The risk of being betrayed was my fear. I portrayed the image of an introvert, which in fact I was not. I would go out of the way to dissuade people from coming very close to me. If they came close enough, there was a risk of getting attached, and again I would go through the entire cycle of betrayal, letdown, and feeling unloved."

"But by being an introvert, you, in any case, remained unloved." The gentle soul of Sarah was compassionate about this paradox of life.

"This is the beauty of the dramas of life. ***The feelings that we try to avoid the most, are the same ones we land up with at the end.*** The seeds of a mango tree can only manifest a tree, which in turn will produce mango seeds in multiples."

Arun was muttering softly in self-introspection. For a change he was preaching to himself.

"The same is true for me. At a certain level I did not want to feel worthless. But every time I tried running away from it, I ended up feeling 'poor me' and felt worthless once again."

"That is the case with Dipti too. She also fights very hard not to feel deprived. But most of the time, she makes people around her so insecure and defensive, that eventually their reaction and response make her feel deprived." Sarah spoke with a compassionate understanding of Dipti's life.

Arun felt he had some confession to make. He stopped walking and stared into her eyes with deep honesty and integrity. "When your indifference became very painful for me to take, after much introspection I realized that your behaviour is the result of my own belief. You had no choice but to play this role because my beliefs would not let you play any other role. And interestingly I realized that I had to play another game of feeling complete within.

That's what made a huge change in your attitude overnight."

"Gosh! I just lost the credit of being an understanding wife," Sarah joked as she felt a bit uncomfortable with the seriousness of this conversation. But Arun remained serious.

"No, Sarah. It is by being who you are, that you have helped me discover myself."

The closest people in our lives are like mirrors reflecting our strengths and weaknesses.

"Thanks for everything, Sarah." She simply lowered her eyelids in acknowledgment.

They spent the rest of the journey in each other's arms, oblivious to the world, until the change in the air made them realize that they were already at the Mumbai port and back to reality, to make a great new beginning once again.

Once you drop your games, it is perfectly possible to be who you are and be completely acceptable to the world around you. ***When the world does not accept you the way you are, be sure, somewhere you have not accepted yourself completely. Your world is your display screen. It has no choice but to display the contents within, stored in the form of beliefs and conditioning.***

In a relationship where two people are involved, it is interesting to find out what one gets out of the relationship. The answer indicates the void which could be the driving factor behind the relationship.

Often people get into a relationship to fulfil a certain void in their lives, hoping the void would be fulfilled by the partner. Interestingly the same void comes in the way of a healthy relationship. Most of the time, rather than filling up the void, the partner helps the other one magnify that void.

That is exactly what happened in Sarah and Arun's life, but they were able to bring to awareness the beliefs which were manifesting the void.

Rather than blaming each other, rather than waiting for each other to reciprocate favorably, they chose to work with their own beliefs and personalities, to seek completion within.

Sarah opened her eyes when it was very bright and sunny outside. She marveled at the amazing natural alarm clock that understands the calendar too. The wise little alarm in her mind knew that it was a Sunday and she could have a leisurely start to the day.

Her body longed to have Arun by her side so that she could cuddle in bed a little longer, but the sound of the running water from the shower coming from the bathroom shook her out of her dreamy state.

She wondered why he had rushed for his bath so early. Perhaps he had some urgent meeting which she was not aware of.

Lying in bed, she waited for him to come out, but she kept waiting for more than half an hour.

"Arun," Sarah shouted to find out what happened in the bathroom.

The mind has a tendency to think of the worst possibility first. Sarah's mind was no exception. When Arun did not respond to her loud calling, out of sheer nervousness she tried opening the door, which opened effortlessly.

Thank God he had not locked the door, she thought; peeping inside the bathroom to check what he was doing for such a long time.

He was lying in the bathtub with his eyes closed. The shower was on and the water was overflowing, flooding the bathroom. His body was absolutely motionless. Several thoughts crossed her mind. But she managed to shake them off immediately. She focused on his breathing and realized that he was in a very deep meditative space and did not feel it right to disturb him. She was about to leave when he gestured to her to come closer.

As she placed her hand in his extended palms, he gently pulled her into the bathtub.

“Arun, there is not much space in the tub. I still have my clothes on...look, it’s flooded....”

“Forget all that. Just come inside.”

She managed to settle her butt between his legs and her head resting on his chest. “Sarah, don’t move. Listen to my heartbeats and feel the water sprinkling on your body.”

From his touch Sarah knew that it was not one of those sensuous moods.

He was serious about something. He started opening the buttons of her shirt. She remained completely still.

“Sarah, feel the droplets on your breasts. You’ll love it,” he said, as he tossed aside the light pink silk covering her breasts.

“Nothing is more enjoyable than your lips on my nipple Arun,” Sarah tried arousing him.

“Sarah, let’s be quiet for a while. Let’s meditate on the feel of the water droplets on our skin.”

Sarah knew from his touch that he meant what he said. She remained quiet for a while forgetting the world around her. The entire focus was on his breath, the heartbeat and the water droplets on her chest.

They spent an hour spellbound. “Sarah, God can be felt in such simple experiences of life.”

“Arun, I experience God whenever I am with you.” “Sarah, are you still looking out for a guru?” “Nope. Not anymore.”

“You are my guru who has helped me find the guru within.” She turned in the tub and kissed him on his lips. His hands on her back were reassuring and caressing her at the same time.”

“Sarah, shall I bathe you today?” Sarah marveled at the proposal. This could be a beautiful Sunday morning gift. He gently and carefully undressed her, applied the body wash in masterful strokes on her hands and legs. Then he turned to her private parts and gently rubbed the gel with a lot of love. Sarah felt like a goddess being bathed by a devotee. This unique experience of love and devotion created a beautiful stillness within her. She had never felt any man touching her with such reverence.

“Thanks. Arun, you have awakened the true essence of a woman in me.” “Thanks, Sarah, you have stimulated the true spirit of a man in me.” “I love you.”

“And I love you,” he said while pouring water on her genitals in a meditative space.

As he gently wiped her body with a soft towel, she had tears in her eyes. “Is it possible for any man to be intimate with the woman he loves, and not get sexually aroused? It's so difficult to believe this!

"You are not just a woman for me. You are a Goddess for me because you helped me get in touch with the God within me." He bent down on his knees to kiss her on her navel.

Since time immemorial, men and women have been seeking completion in each other. But they often get lost in their body consciousness. Those who learn to go beyond with an intention to unite with the essence of the partner, find ultimate bliss in the act of union.

Sarah and Arun were fortunate. They were guided souls who felt complete within themselves and in union with each other.

www.ingramcontent.com/pod-product-compliance
Lightning Source LLC
LaVergne TN
LVHW041205150826
845673LV00001B/288

* 9 7 9 8 8 8 8 6 9 9 6 2 1 *